CURVES FOR THE RAKISH DUKE

THE BUSTY BODICE CLUB

CATHY MAXWELL

This book is dedicated to the smart, wonderful authors in the Busty Bodice collaboration: Eliana Piers, Tracy Sumner, Annabelle Anders, Robyn DeHart, Kathleen Ayers, and Janna MacGregor.

I am wealthy in my friends.

ISBN 979-8993094106

Cover Art by Dar Albert

HUMAN AUTHORED

Reg #: 329330, https://authorsguild.org/human

Formatted with Vellum

1

LONDON, 1816

They called him the Dragon of London because they claimed he set women on fire.

Lady Celeste Harrington watched the Duke of Salcombe weave his way through the crowded ballroom, and she believed every word they said about him. Oliver Granier was the most physically handsome man she had ever seen in her seven and twenty years. He moved with a deadly grace. He knew all eyes followed him, most out of envy, some out of spite. He believed in his worth and Celeste couldn't help but feel a touch of jealousy.

The duke might also be Celeste's last chance of fulfilling the task her late father had given her, that of setting up a charity. It was proving more difficult than she had imagined. It took money and a great deal of social influence to establish a charity. Celeste had little of the former and none of the latter.

But with the Dragon's help, that could change.

The duke paused in front of a hallway that led to a very quiet library. Her heart quickened. He must have received her note. He was going to meet her. She had sent the note anonymously, of course. She'd also not explained her purpose. No good could come from tipping her hand too quickly. And it might be that he had just happened to pause in front of that hall. . . but Celeste didn't believe in happenstance.

He surveyed the glittering, noisy crowd, nodding here and there to those who caught his attention. A willowy young matron blushed. A silver-haired dowager gave him a saucy wink back. Men followed his eye to see what beauties he'd discovered.

Celeste knew he didn't see her. She was rarely noticed. In a family of eight proud and beautiful sisters, she was the one usually overlooked. Perhaps her father had given her such a herculean assignment because he had known how difficult it would be for Celeste to be in charge of anything. She preferred to be home with her knitting needles, her garden, her cat, and her dogs. She adored dogs.

However, as her father wrote, *You have a tender heart. Use it to help others. Create a charity that will help you right some of the wrongs in this world.*

The challenge spoke to her soul. And because her father had shown in his last request that he believed in her, she had come to London to set right an egregious wrong she believed must be changed. One that was huge and glaring. One she would truly need a dragon's help to set right.

The duke turned and strode purposefully down the hall. He was heading for the library. He was going to meet with her. Her daring, daring plan was now set into motion.

Almost panicked, Celeste looked around for her friend Dame Beatrice. Bea was thirty years older than her seven and twenty, but the only person other than her twin, Georgiana, whom Celeste trusted to help. By meeting with a renowned rake as the duke privately in such a social setting,

Celeste knew she flirted with scandal. However, how else was she to talk to him? She couldn't knock on the door to his residence and they had no friends in common. Requesting a meeting anonymously had been her only choice.

Bea noticed Celeste's summons. She bowed out of her conversation with friends and worked her way through the crowd. "Has he taken the bait?" she whispered conspiratorially.

"He has." With a casualness she was far from feeling, Celeste led her friend across the ballroom and down the hall leading to the library. They strolled as if admiring the portraits lining the walls. When they came in sight of the closed library door, Celeste said, "Stand guard where you can see the ballroom and yet be close enough to warn me if we are about to be interrupted."

"How shall I do that?" Bea asked. "A hand signal?"

"The door will be closed for privacy."

"I could shout a warning."

"That might not be wisest."

"Well, how shall I warn you?" Bea demanded, the ostrich feathers in her hair bouncing with indignation.

Celeste chewed on the problem a moment and then replied, "Greet the person as if you are friends and talk so loudly that I will hear you through the door. That will be my warning to—" She stopped. She didn't actually know what she would do. Perhaps jump out a window? Hide behind the furniture? "It will all work out."

Bea wasn't convinced. "Are you certain this is wise? I hear tell the Dragon has a temper."

Celeste had heard that as well. They said he could be

quite humorless when crossed, or when he felt some marriage-minded miss was trying to entrap him. Apparently, many had tried. Well, he had nothing to worry about on that score from her. "He's my last chance to see this charity established, Bea. It is a risk I must take." She gave her friend a quick squeeze, walked over to the door, and, with a glance over her shoulder to ensure no one was watching, opened it.

OLIVER WAS IN A GRUMPY MOOD.

He'd just had words with Prime Minister Liverpool, and in front of Robinson, no less. They had rejected his ideas without really giving him a hearing. They'd told him to focus on his seat in the Lords and not think too much. Change happened slowly, they'd said. Britain needed to recover from the war. They couldn't stir the pot too quickly.

Oliver could see so many things about his country and his government that needed changing, that he wanted to stir the pot with an oar. And, no, he did not wish to cool his heels until someone needed his vote. He believed his input in the planning was equally valuable. He had ideas, fresh ones, and he hated being patronized—because *that* was what they had done. Without speaking the words, they had let him know they considered him...frivolous.

The library was lit by a small fire in the hearth. He pulled the missive from the inside pocket of his evening jacket. The handwriting was definitely feminine: *Please meet me in the library at your earliest convenience to discuss a matter for your urgent consideration.*

Urgent consideration. He smiled grimly. He understood what that meant. Women begged for his favor. He hated being pursued. It made him feel exactly the way Liverpool and Robinson perceived him.

And yet, here he was, because he really had nowhere else to go. He had little family and few friends. Perhaps he *was* as idle and shallow as his peers thought him? But that was not the man he wished to be.

The room suddenly felt over-warm. He crossed to a window, pulled back the heavy drapes, undid the latch, and lifted the sash. Outside, the early summer night hummed with voices and laughter on the nearby terrace, despite it being unseasonably cool.

On the morrow, the papers would ask where the Duke of Salcombe had gone off to in the middle of a ball. What beauty had captured his attention? There was one correspondent who seemed to delight in asking, "Whom did the Dragon have in his lair?"

Oliver hated the nickname.

He *was* changing, he told himself. Liverpool might dismiss him as lacking intellectual depth, but he was wrong. Oliver just needed the opportunity to prove his mettle.

So, why was he standing in his host's library, waiting for some lovely to reveal herself? He'd stopped clandestine assignations a month or so ago.

It was her scent.

He lifted the note to his nose. The perfume had caught him by surprise. It was not a cloying floral scent as was the fashion. No, it was light with promise. Cherries, a hint of almond, the barest whiff of rose. He could breathe this scent forever. It beckoned him. It stirred his jaded curiosity. He pictured the writer tucking this note into the décolleté of her gown. Letting it rest against her breast.

Oliver lowered the note. Now, he was being ridiculously romantic, and he was not a romantic man.

The door handle turned. She had arrived.

Despite being curiously anxious to meet his mysterious admirer, he stepped back against the curtains instead of moving forward. A crack of light from the hallway slid across the walls as the door opened...but instead of a tall, willowy creature, a petite figure slid into the room. He had the impression of a full, buxom chest and the very feminine curve of hips. The hearth's fire highlighted artfully arranged, ale-colored curls. As she quietly closed the door, he experienced a stab of disappointment. He was a tall man and liked a woman to be of a certain height. This miss merely came up to his chest.

She looked around the room for him. Her eyes were wide, and he could almost hear the excited beating of her heart as if struck by her own audacity. In that moment, he knew she wasn't some practiced seductress, but an innocent. The scent's promise had betrayed him. He'd expected someone more alluring.

The chit didn't notice him immediately. Probably because his dark evening clothes helped him fit into the shadows. So, he let her know he was there.

"If your intent was a bit of debauchery," he said, enjoying how his deep voice startled her as she whirled to face him, "I am sorry to disappoint you. I don't seduce virgins."

Instead of blushing or being ashamed of her brazen behavior, she answered, "That is good to know. I shall let down my guard. Then again, I am no miss just out of the school room. Perhaps you fear being compromised by me? Or 'debauched?' Such a silly word. I don't even like the sound of it."

And in that moment, just that easily, Oliver was charmed. What an interesting, courageous little mouse she was. Soft and round and buxom with the most extraordinary eyes. Their large, almond shape reflected the firelight like twin flames. Seconds before, he'd been cataloguing her faults. He now noticed her assets. Beyond her obvious endowments, her skin was perfect, with just a hint of rosy blush, as if she were far too aware of how forward she was being and could not help herself.

She was also very well dressed in her soft green silk. Her gloves were of good kidskin and the hairpins holding her curls in place had jeweled tips.

Then, from across the room, he caught a hint of her scent, the same as that of the notepaper. His blood quickened. Perhaps he *was* ready for a little debauchery...

But first, "Who are you, little mouse?"

Her nose scrunched with distaste as if she didn't like nicknames either. "I am Lady Celeste Harrington. My brother is the Duke of Kenbrooks."

"I don't know Kenbrooks. I've heard of him, but our paths have never crossed. However, I am certain he would not be happy to know I am alone in our host's library with his sister."

"Being a rake must be very tiresome."

She was right. Still, he couldn't admit it. "The ladies like it," he replied.

Lady Celeste hummed a noncommittal sound that snapped Oliver out of his good humor, especially on the heels of Liverpool's dismissal. "If you aren't interested in an assignation, then *why* did you summon me here?"

"Because I have been observing you, Your Grace." She clasped her gloved hands in front of her like a soprano preparing to warble. "I think I know what you need."

He folded his arms. "And what, pray tell, is that?"

"A chance to reform."

2

Celeste didn't know how she had expected the duke to receive her offer, but it was not to tilt back his head and have a good, long laugh.

The strong, masculine sound filled the room. She waited for him to finish, her back tight.

At last, he regained control over himself, and the room fell silent. His sharp gaze reassessed her. She felt there wasn't a hair or thread he didn't notice. Here was the Dragon, the man women whispered about. She recognized his power even before he said in a voice as smooth as syrup and just as thick with promise, "What if I don't wish to reform, Lady Celeste?"

She didn't answer. She couldn't. Her mouth had gone suddenly dry while other parts of her tightened in anticipation. He walked toward her, stopping when they were almost toe to toe. She fought the urge to step back. She had to look up to meet his eye.

His lips curved into a most wicked smile. "What lessons could you teach me?" he wondered as if he already knew the answer.

She swallowed for courage and said, "Not the ones you seem to be thinking of."

"How do you know what I'm thinking?"

"You have a reputation."

He shook his head as if slightly disappointed and took a step back. "Very well, you aren't looking for seduction, and you haven't run in fear or swooned into my arms. I appreciate that. Swooning females are tiresome."

"I imagine swooning males are equally annoying."

His lips twitched as if he stifled a smile. "I wouldn't know."

"I do. Indiscriminate swooning is a bane for all involved."

He gave a sharp bark of laugher as if she had surprised him. "Quite true." He gave her a small bow of respect, and his manner changed to one of respect. "So, what do you wish of me, my lady?"

"A moment of your time. It is impossible for a woman, especially a single woman of our class, to speak to an unmarried gentleman without the gossips having the wrong idea. I couldn't knock on your door. We don't have any acquaintances in common." She shrugged. "This seemed to be the only way to make contact, and if someone were to walk in right now, it could be awkward. Would you please sit, Your Grace? You are tall, and I tire of looking up at you."

Without argument, he did exactly as she asked. He walked to the chair in front of the fire and plopped down. He held out his gloved hands, a sign that he was at her disposal.

She moved between his chair and its footstool to stand in front of him. "I would like you to become the chief patron of my charity."

"Me?" He eyed her suspiciously. "Involved with a charity? Are you certain you wouldn't rather be seduced?"

Celeste made an impatient sound. "I'm being serious."

"I am, too."

"Your Grace, I am making an earnest request. However, if you are not interested, say as much and I will happily leave." She threw the last words out with a hint of bravado, although her greatest fear was that he would reject her offer.

He shook his head. "If it is a charity, a wiser course would be to solicit Lady Redhill's assistance. Isn't she the maven of charities amongst the *ton*?" She heard the hint of distaste in his tone. It was rumored that he and the powerful Lady Redhill despised each other. Another reason Celeste had come to him.

"I went to Lady Redhill. She laughed at me. She dismissed my idea as 'unimportant.' And you are right that everyone in Society turns to her for approval. If I had a shilling for every time I've been asked if I have discussed this proposal with Lady Redhill, I wouldn't need to raise money."

"Rejected by Lady Redhill. You truly are desperate then."

"I am."

"But you know one person who isn't afraid of her power," he said confidently.

"You," she answered. "I am hoping you will hear me out and agree to help."

"I'd agree to help just to tweak her ladyship's nose. However, go on. What is this charity you want me to sponsor?"

This was the question she had prayed to hear. Proprieties flew from her mind in her enthusiasm to gain his support. She sat on the footstool, ready to sway him to her cause.

LADY CELESTE'S expressive eyes filled with sincerity and a hope kindred to desire, and Oliver found himself wishing she did want to be seduced. The hearth light haloed her golden curls and highlighted the curves of very generous breasts and the beckoning shadow of her cleavage.

Oliver knew he should not even be encouraging her. Without Lady Redhill's blessing, her cause was hopeless.

However, he was curious about what she was planning. Her passion for her cause shone bright in her eyes, and that cherry and rose scent swirled around her like some siren's spell.

"I want to help our soldiers who have been severely wounded by the war. Many men have lost an arm or a leg, or been blinded. There are men who have no family to help care for them. They end up begging on the streets."

Oliver gave a start. She had surprised him. He had been anticipating a decorated box for the poor or a garden project with a statue in some park. Even a home for motherless children. That was the purview of gently reared young ladies.

Not men who had been destroyed by war.

He understood Lady Redhill's disapproval. Such a cause was not proper for gentlewomen.

Except... was it true their country had abandoned wounded soldiers? If so, that was outrageous.

He leaned forward. "Don't our soldiers receive a pension for such devastating injuries?"

"That is what I thought. But I have since learned that the pension they receive is a pittance. Also, many feel deformed. They had strong bodies, but now that they are without an arm or a leg, they can no longer do the work they once did. And they are alone. Often by choice. One man told me he is so ashamed of his injury that he didn't want to return to his village."

Teasing and seduction evaporated from Oliver's mind. He pictured himself in these circumstances. He, too, would feel less of a man.

"They deserve a good place to live," she continued. "I want to build a community for them instead of leaving them on the streets of London."

This was truly a noble cause. He nodded his agreement, his mind beginning to work on the problem.

"And many dogs and cats on the streets of London need homes as well."

Oliver stopped nodding, suddenly confused by the change of topic. "Dogs and cats?"

"Have you not noticed the soldiers begging on our streets?"

He hadn't. But now that she prodded him, he reflected that there were a number of crippled beggars on the streets. He'd never suspected they could be former soldiers. "But dogs and cats?"

She smiled at him as if she knew how woefully unaware he was. "Every time you see one of the king's men begging, he always has a beloved animal at his side. A dog or a cat. One man has a crow that he has trained. These animals are like family to the men, so wherever we find a place for them to live, the animals must be included. A place in the country would be ideal. Someplace large enough that the men can take care of themselves and regain a sense of self-respect. You do appreciate the importance of pets, don't you?"

He didn't... but he didn't wish to tell her that. She obviously had strong opinions on the subject. He was also beginning to understand why Lady Redhill laughed.

And then it hit him—the Harrington sisters. Yes, he'd heard of them. One codger at his club had claimed they were all too intelligent and forward-thinking for their own good. The man had also added a dire verdict, "No wonder they aren't married."

Oliver was aware that there were numerous women with excellent minds, spirit, and even looks who never married. His cousin Amanda came to mind. She'd rather have her books, art, and garden than an overbearing husband.

"I need your help, Your Grace." Lady Celeste leaned forward, seemingly unaware that it drew his attention to the mounds of lovely, smooth skin above her bodice. It was hard not to stare, especially since he found himself drawn to her. However, Amanda had taught him that women didn't appreciate being ogled. He reluctantly forced his gaze to meet Lady Celeste's imploring eyes. "And I can help you in return," she promised. "It would be good for your reputation to be seen as *noble*. A noble duke."

Now she had his complete attention. "Instead of… what?" Was he not noble? Was he not a duke? Then he thought of the way Liverpool and Robinson had dismissed him.

"Please, I don't mean to insult you," she hurried to say. "You are an important guest on any list. However, I believe you are being invited for the gossip. People like to pretend they are scandalized by the number of women you have bedded—"

"Not that many women. I'm discerning."

"Perhaps," she conceded without so much as a blush. "It may all be jealousy or the enjoyment of spreading rumors.

Did you truly swing across Lady Milbury's ballroom on her chandelier, showering wax on everyone?"

"That was years ago. I was barely nineteen. And I did it for a wager. I won. Unfortunately, that damn story follows me everywhere." He made a frustrated sound. "Most of what the papers print is untrue."

"If you support my charity, it will show a different side to you. People will think of you as a leader."

She was right, but he'd learned to be wary. "What do you receive out of my patronage?"

"Your endorsement will attract attention. People will listen to you."

"But you, what do *you* receive?"

"My late father's last request was for me to start a charity for a cause that matters to me. If I succeed, I will receive a small inheritance, one I will donate to the charity."

He wanted to say yes, but he hesitated. Lady Redhill, with her sniffs of disdain and rolling of eyes, was one of his chief critics, and her opinion carried weight. She enjoyed belittling people. Perhaps she was behind some of Liverpool's concerns about him? He knew why she was angry with him. She had wanted him to marry her daughter. She'd practically thrown the girl at him. And he'd been too young back then to understand how he could have better handled the situation.

But he was older now. He was also ready to stand for something. Lady Celeste's cause was just... until she rattled on about dogs and cats. However, he questioned if his association with the charity, especially considering Lady Celeste's unmarried status, would do more harm than good—

Voices sounded right outside the library door. *Women's*

voices. Loud women's voices. One was practically shouting, and the other raised her voice to answer.

Lady Celeste's eyes widened. "That sounds like Lady Redhill. I *must* hide." She jumped up from the stool, just as Oliver rose.

The two actions were ill-timed. They collided. Legs became tangled and almost toppled them to the floor. Their arms grabbed each other as they attempted to save themselves from falling. Her breasts pressed against his chest. Full, lovely breasts, he noted, but there was no time to savor the moment because Lady Redhill answered the woman in the hall with an impervious, "I go where I please. Stand aside, Dame Beatrice, or I shall elbow you back."

The library door slammed open, and Oliver took the only action that made sense to him. He swung Lady Celeste around in his arms so that she was hidden in the shelter of his body, his back toward the door. He did the most logical thing for a man and a woman to do in a firelit room.

He kissed her.

3

She was being *kissed* by the *Dragon*.

Celeste's brain spun with the realization.

And he was very, very good at kissing. He had *earned* his reputation. This kiss was beyond anything Celeste's fevered imagination could have conjured. His mouth perfectly fit hers.

On a sane and practical level, she understood he was shielding her identity in the only obvious way Lady Redhill or anyone else would believe. He might even be attempting to protect his reputation as well. Men didn't seduce the Harrington sisters.

That didn't mean she couldn't enjoy the experience.

She lifted herself on her tiptoes so she could meet his kiss. She liked being enveloped in the warmth of his body. His clothes smelled of sandalwood, soap, and maleness.

Her lips melded against his. She couldn't stop them. Or prevent herself from leaning closer to his strength. He was a solid, muscular wall providing a haven from Lady Redhill's gossip and possible ruin. Not that she was particularly worried about those things right now. She was enjoying the kiss too much.

As if from a distance, she caught the sound of Dame Beatrice chastising Lady Redhill for barging in on the couple. Meanwhile, his hand found her waist. Had he purposely placed it there? She liked the weight of his touch even as it pulled her intimately closer. A new, more intriguing desire began to build. She breathed him in—

He broke off the kiss.

For the space of a heartbeat, Celeste tried to follow his lips. But then, with what sounded like very real annoyance, he barked out, "What is going on?" His arm tightened around her so that her face smooshed against his white shirt and black, patterned silk waistcoat.

"Leading astray another young lovely, Your Grace?" Lady Redhill asked with a snide sniff.

Reality, in the form of her ladyship's voice, raised its ugly head. Celeste came to her senses. Was a kiss enough to make her family the topic of gossip for ages to come? The duke's hand prevented her from bolting.

"What I do is not your concern, my lady," the duke drawled. "Now leave us."

Lady Redhill did not obey. She turned to Beatrice. "I wonder why *you* were standing guard?"

"I-I wasn't standing guard," Beatrice stuttered in annoyance. "I just saw no reason for you to be in the library."

"Next, you will be telling me the Duke of Salcombe was sitting in the dark, reading."

"He does read," Beatrice said as if offended for His Grace.

"Although I prefer *other* activities in the dark," the duke corrected in a lazy, silky voice. "Now, begone, Lady Redhill. Go find your fellow petty hens and tell them what you saw.

It will not be news. You tell me often that I already have a wicked reputation."

"But the woman you are with?" her ladyship hedged.

"Is my affair."

There was a long, combative silence.

Celeste tried to relax. It was difficult. Her mind reeled at the horror of possible outcomes—although that kiss might have been worth the ruin.

Then, Lady Redhill conceded stiffly, "I do beg your pardon, Your Grace. I should not interfere with your 'sport.' Come, Dame Beatrice. Let us enjoy a walk down the hall."

The door closed, and Celeste's knees almost buckled. Fortunately, the duke still had his arm around her waist. He turned and sat her in his chair. She gratefully relaxed until she realized he was furious, the lines of his face harsh in the hearth light.

"Was all *this* a scheme to trap me into marriage?" he snapped.

His anger stunned her. "No, *no*, my only purpose was to ask you to support my charity."

"Did you know the woman who brought Lady Redhill here?"

"She is Dame Beatrice, and she is my friend. She was my lookout in case someone like Lady Redhill became nosy."

His stance didn't soften. "She isn't good at her job."

"She slowed Lady Redhill down," Celeste pointed out. "And now, I believe I should leave." Especially after that kiss. She was still dazed over it. She stood, thankful her legs now held her weight, and would have walked out the door, except he stopped her.

"Lady Redhill is outside. She will wait for someone to leave this room and then pounce on them."

This sounded like something the woman would do. "Why does she dislike you so much?"

"Because she and her daughter attempted to trap me into marriage, but I escaped. They had to settle on Alton instead. He doesn't have the money I have, and well, he's Alton." Lord Alton was universally reviled as a bore with very bad breath.

Celeste frowned. "What do we do? We must leave this room eventually. We can't outwait her."

"There is always an exit." He walked over to one of the room's large windows. It had already been cracked open. He lifted the sash higher, then offered his hand. "My lady?"

Celeste glanced at the door and realized he was right. Lady Redhill would do anything to know whom he had been kissing. Celeste crossed to him and took his hand. He swept her up as if she weighed nothing and dropped her gently into the garden, the earth soft beneath her slippers.

He jumped down beside her.

Not far, on the other side of a clump of clipped evergreens, was a terrace along the back of the house. Guests were milling about there, laughing and enjoying themselves.

"Join them," he ordered.

"What of you?"

"I have other plans."

"You're leaving the ball?"

"I'm leaving." He still sounded angry.

Wishing to keep the peace between them, she said, "I am certain you have a right to be distrustful of women, but not of me. I sincerely want you to help with my charity. I have no other motive"

The duke made a noncommittal sound.

The reaction annoyed her. "I am not responsible for

Lady Redhill's animosity toward you. However, I do need you to be the lead patron of my charity. There is no other sponsor who will attract subscribers the way I know you can. To be honest, Lady Redhill will do everything in her power to see that I don't succeed since I am acting without her approval."

Another grunt.

Celeste felt her temper sizzle. "Your Grace, please—"

"*Stop,*" he commanded. "I don't know what I'm going to do. Your request is unusual and I don't know how I feel about the matter. However, I wish to be alone now. Can you see your way over to the terrace and rejoin the ball? It would be awkward if we were seen together."

"Yes, of course I can," Celeste replied, chastened.

Before Lady Redhill had barged in, she had been hopeful for his patronage. Now, she sensed he held her responsible for her ladyship's brashness. It was unfair, but the decision to help was his—unfortunately. "Let me know what you decide," she said, dismissing him as bluntly as he had dismissed her.

She started walking toward the path leading to the terrace. In spite of her pride, she could not resist one backward glance at him. He'd taught her many things this evening, one of them being how potent a kiss could truly be except, the duke no longer stood where she'd left him. He had disappeared into the garden's shadows.

4

Oliver let himself out through a back gate. He strode down the passageway and out onto a side street. He didn't bother fetching his hat. It was more important that he moved.

This had been a devil of a night—from his dismissal by Liverpool and Robinson, to Lady Redhill's spitefulness, to Lady Celeste's request for him to be the lead patron of her non-existent charity. It galled him that Lady Celeste might be the only person to take him seriously.

His mind churned with angry thoughts. He wasn't heading home. He didn't care where he went or that the streets were growing darker. After all, he was the *Dragon*, a bit of silliness that had once made him feel—what? Accepted? Safe? That was a laugh.

His old companions were marrying, having families, and being respected. Many drank his wine while making snide comments behind his back. They saw him as that wild, fatherless youth who had come into his title way too young.

But he was changing. He felt it deep inside. He just didn't know what he was changing into. Or what *he* wanted.

His thoughts fell on Lady Celeste. Her zeal for her cause had shone in her eyes. She had risked her reputation to approach him... because she had been right. There weren't many ways a single woman could publicly seek him out.

Of course, if he did support this charity of hers, he could become the laughingstock of London. A charity for wounded soldiers and their pets. Pets? It was silly. The sort of thing a woman would dream up.

Still, he envied her passion—

A dog's snarl was his first warning. He heard the sound and stopped. He was unarmed and had a healthy respect for angry dogs.

Oliver looked around. He was not far from Covent Garden but on the poorer side of this section of the city. The hour was late. No lights shone from windows. All was quiet save the dog's low growl.

Then, to Oliver's alarm, one of the shadows seemed to rise and take the shape of a man. He had apparently been asleep, huddled against a building's brick facade. The dog began barking.

"Here now, Pistol. Quiet now." The raspy-voiced man leaned against the wall. "Sorry, sir. He's a protective one."

A coach turned a corner and passed by. Light from the vehicle's lanterns fell upon them. The man was a beggar who had apparently made his bed for the night on the street. The pup, a dirty, white, matted terrier, had been standing guard.

Oliver's attention landed on the man's crutch. He was missing a leg.

"How did you lose your limb?" Oliver demanded.

"King's Service, if it matters to you."

This was one of the men Lady Celeste wished to help.

Pistol growled as if warning Oliver to ask no more questions. "Don't mind him, sir. Pistol looks out for me. Or so he thinks." The man had a Northern accent. He was of slight build but wiry and tough.

Oliver's boot pushed a plate on the ground. There were a few coins on it. He reached into his waistcoat pocket where he kept money for vails. He dropped coins on the plate.

"Thank you, sir. Thank you."

"Are you always here?"

"Most times, unless we get run off."

"Don't you have any lodgings?"

"Lodgings?" The man laughed. "Aye, lodgings. Because I like living on the street, eh?"

"But you are a Northerner. Why are you in London?"

There was a long pause. Then, the man said, "I'd be a burden to them up there. I was a woodsman. Can't travel the forest on one leg. Can't swing an axe when I need at least one arm to hold me crutch."

"Don't you receive a pension?"

The man spit his opinion of the king's pension. "Barely enough to matter. I see that it goes to me daughter and her family. My wife left me a long time ago. Didn't want to wait for a soldier. Doubt if she would want a cripple for a husband. Has a new man now."

Oliver was humbled by how completely this man had been shut out of his old life. In that moment, he even understood the importance of a loyal little dog, one who didn't appear to be any better fed than his master. "What is your name?"

"William Dryer, sir."

"If I told you to come with me, William Dryer, would you leave your dog behind?"

"Absolutely not. He is faithful to me, and I to him."

"Then bring your dog. Let's go."

"Go where?" William asked suspiciously.

"Someplace with a roof and off the street. There will be food, too. Good food."

"I don't take charity."

Oliver studied the man leaning against the wall on one leg, all of his worldly possessions in a ragged bundle on the ground. Lady Celeste had been correct. William Dryer and all the others like him needed to feel whole and as if they paid their own way. They were proud men who had served their country. "I'm not offering charity, but work." He had no idea what the man could do—but he'd wager Lady Celeste might. "Do you come, or not?"

"Why would you do this, sir? Look at me."

"I see you. Come, or not. The choice is yours." Oliver began walking. A beat later, he slowed his step as he heard Dryer moving behind him. The soldier used his crutch with one hand and carried his meager possessions in the other.

Oliver soon learned that traveling with a cripple was slow going. He held out his hand as an offer to help Dryer carry his bundle, but the man proudly ignored it.

Pistol didn't seem to mind the slow pace. He marched beside his master, even pausing when Dryer had to readjust his crutch under his arm. The animal's devotion and awareness surprised Oliver.

His family had never had pets. His mother hadn't liked them. They'd had hunting hounds. Packs of them at his various estates. They were wild, mad, howling dogs that were more interested in scaring up pheasants than in what their humans were doing. He doubted if even one of them would worry about his well-being.

Eventually, they reached Oliver's stables, where he tasked the night groom with seeing to Dryer's comfort. As

Oliver was leaving, he overheard Dryer ask the groom who he was. "That is His Grace, the Duke of Salcombe."

"Bloody hell," Dryer whispered, and Oliver could not help but smile.

Bloody hell was right. He'd just done something positive, something that might change another man's life.

His view of the world shifted inside him, a change of attitude. In the silence of the night, he realized he felt good about himself. He could barely remember a time when he'd been proud of who he was.

And he owed this change to Lady Celeste Harrington, who had chosen him to lead her charity. *To lead*. He could be *the* leader.

He went to bed filled with new purpose. Lady Celeste would be very pleased with his decision. She'd looked so worried when he'd left her in the garden, and it made him rather happy that he could alleviate her fears regarding her charity. He wasn't certain what he would do with Dryer and Pistol, but she would know. He'd discuss the matter with her in the morning.

When Oliver woke, his new sense of purpose was stronger than ever.

He sat with his secretary, Peters, a man who always had good ideas. He told him about the charity and his decision to become its Lead Patron.

"I believe, Your Grace, that a notice in the papers of your patronage would not be out of order."

"Yes, good idea. See to it."

"What is the name of the charity, Your Grace?"

Oliver searched his memory. Had Lady Celeste told him

the name of the charity? If she had, he didn't remember. Very well, he would create one.

He thought a moment. "Legless Soldiers" would be a terrible name. "For King and Country" sounded important, but what did it mean?

Then, an idea hit him. "The charity is called 'Our Brave Soldiers.'" He liked the sound of it. He thought men like Dryer would as well. No talk of cripples. Lady Celeste would probably want to add "and Pets," but that didn't matter. Once it was printed in all the papers, the title would be as he deemed fit.

Nor did he anticipate a problem. He was making the right decisions. Unfortunately, he and Peters became so busy with the planning, he lost track of time. He had promised to help his friend Haskell look at a horse. Later, they'd indulged in a good dinner at an inn with an excellent cellar.

Tomorrow. He would call on Lady Celeste first thing, and she'd be pleased with all he had accomplished.

However, as he fell asleep, he was surprised that his last thought wasn't of plans and charities, or even the excellent horseflesh he had convinced Haskell to purchase. No, he found himself recalling the feel of Lady Celeste in his arms, of fully feminine curves pressed snugly against him, and of lips that not only yielded to him, but made demands of their own.

And though he reminded himself—one more time—that Lady Celeste was not the sort of female who attracted him, that he liked statuesque, willowy women, the memory of the passion for her cause in her almond-shaped eyes wound their way through his dreams.

5

Celeste had spent the previous day pacing the floor of her sitting room, waiting and hoping for some word from the duke. Even though their parting had not given her cause to believe he would agree to helping with her charity, she'd held out hope that he might reconsider.

By nightfall, she had accepted that his answer was no. Dispirited, she had stayed in for the evening and was surprised to fall into a deep, exhausted sleep. All of her energy of late had gone toward fulfilling her father's last request of her, and she had failed.

The next morning, she revealed what she'd done to her twin, Georgiana, confessing that she had finagled a meeting with the duke at the Jensen ball. They had both not yet gone down to break their fast.

"The Duke of Salcombe was my last hope. He is the only one with the courage to flout Lady Redhill. If he were willing to support my charity, I would have heard from him by now."

"Only a day has passed. He might still be thinking about

the matter," George, Celeste's nickname for her twin, said sympathetically.

Celeste shook her head. "He is a suspicious man. He thought I was attempting to trap him into marriage—as if I would marry such an arrogant beast."

"Wait, why would he think you had set up a marriage trap? We don't even know him."

"It is Lady Redhill's fault. She interrupted us while I was asking for his help so he jumped to the conclusion that I had orchestrated some scheme."

George drew in her breath with alarm. "What did she say? Are you a scandal?"

"No, because he kissed me and—"

"*What*? Wait. Hold right here. You were kissed by the Dragon?" George didn't hide her incredulity.

"It wasn't anything special," Celeste claimed with a dismissive wave. "He was trying to protect my identity from Lady Redhill. And he took the correct action. She has no idea I was the woman in the library with him. Except once she left, he accused *me* of trying to entrap him into marriage. I informed him I only wished him to be the lead patron of my charity, but he ran off without a word—"

"*Stop*." George raised her palms. "Or at least take a breath."

Celeste recognized her sister's good advice. She did need to breathe. She and George were not identical twins. They didn't even think alike. But she trusted George more than any other person in the world, save for Beatrice.

Into the sudden void, George said, "Here is the important fact. The Dragon of London *kissed* you."

"He had no choice. I told you, he was trying to protect my identity from Lady Redhill."

George's eyes narrowed. "And kissing you accomplished exactly what, Cece?"

Celeste made an impatient sound. "It created a good reason for why he was in a dark library, alone with a woman. It wasn't a kiss that he meant."

George considered this. "He couldn't just shove you behind a chair or a curtain?"

"There wasn't time. But it was all for naught because he isn't interested in supporting my charity."

"Enough about your charity," George answered. "Is he a good kisser?"

Now, that was a question. There had been moments since the ball when the memory of that kiss threatened Celeste's sanity, but she wasn't about to confess that to her sister. "It was meaningless," she informed George primly. "What concerns me is that I will not be able to honor Father's last request. He believed I could do this, and instead, I've failed"

A knock on their bedroom door interrupted them. Rodman, their butler, announced, "The Duke of Salcombe is here to see you, Lady Celeste."

George's eyes widened in amazement. "Never see him again? And this is early for a call."

"I have no idea why he is here."

Another knock. "Lady Celeste?"

"Please tell him I shall be down momentarily," Celeste said calmly, but inside, panic seized her. She turned to the looking glass. She appeared pale. And should she change from the simple blue day dress she was wearing? Or pin up her hair?

George rose from the bed and crossed the bedroom to open the door.

"Where are you going?" Celeste asked.

"One of us should greet him. Besides, you will need a chaperone."

Her words were the impetus Celeste needed to move. "No, I don't," she informed her twin as she hurried to beat her down the hall to the staircase. "He is calling on a matter of business importance. This isn't a social call."

"No one will believe that," George tossed over her shoulder as she bounced down the steps.

Celeste kept pace with her. "He isn't interested in me."

"He kissed you."

"He was forced to."

"Cece, no one forces a man to kiss a woman."

"It wasn't his choice."

"Mm-hmm," her twin answered as they turned on the last landing before the entrance hall, and then they both came to a halt.

No duke cooled his heels in their foyer. He must be in the receiving room. In silent agreement, they lifted their chins and then regally took the last steps side-by-side, like the gentlewomen they were. They moved to the door of the receiving room.

Still no duke.

"Where did he go?" George whispered.

And then Celeste heard a low-throated sound of masculine appreciation coming from the direction of the family breakfast room. The scent of beef and ham wafted down the hall toward them, a beckoning if ever there was one. Her brother was not in residence. It could be a servant, but she thought not.

She marched down the hall, George at her heels, and strode into the private room to see the Duke of Salcombe opening the covers to the array of breakfast dishes on the sideboard and helping himself to small nibbles with his ungloved fingers. He looked more handsome than ever in the room's late morning sun, his blue-black hair ruffled into wild curls as if he'd just been out riding.

He smiled in greeting, brushing off his fingers, as if he was very pleased to see her. It was a good smile. A winsome one.

Under her breath, George whispered, "Oh, my."

Oh, my, indeed.

Celeste struggled not to show how happy she was to see him, or to recall how she had enjoyed being pressed against his chest the other night. Even from where she stood, she caught the hint of sandalwood and soap. She gathered her wits and asked, "Does this mean you will be my charity's lead patron?"

"Absolutely," he said, and in that moment, Celeste felt as if the heavens had opened and the angels were singing. He was going to help her. She was going to succeed, and she was humbly grateful. In fact, she was so appreciative, she was in danger of weeping with relief.

Rodman entered through the pantry with a tankard of ale for the duke. Salcombe smiled at the offering. "Your chef is excellent," he said. "I've never tasted beef with such flavor. And it is tender. I like tender beef."

Celeste covertly caught a tear before it escaped and embarrassed her. "I shall tell Cook. She will be flattered." She turned to her sister. "I'm certain you have something you should be doing, George?" It was a pointed hint.

"Nothing is more important than chaperoning you, dear sister." George walked up to the duke, who was hovering around a dish of bacon. "I'm Lady Georgiana. However, please, call me George, and did you really kiss my twin last night?"

"*George*." Celeste could have happily murdered her

sister, especially when the duke ducked his head as if to hide his embarrassment. "I'm sorry, Your Grace. George has terrible manners."

"The better to chaperone you, Cece," George replied, unrepentant.

"I don't need a chaperone."

"Obviously, you do if you are kissing a duke at a ball," George whispered brightly.

The duke made a humming sound as he piled a plate high with bacon and beef. "Did you tell her *all* of it?" He carried his food over to the table where he'd set his tankard. "Including Lady Redhill?"

"I did. But Georgiana is a troublemaker."

"That is what sisters are for," George assured her blithely.

"Well, you needn't worry, and please, leave us. His Grace and I have much to discuss."

"Yes, about Our Brave Soldiers."

Celeste frowned, confused. "Our what?"

"Our Brave Soldiers. It's the name I've given to the charity. I had my man Peters send out announcements of my patronage to all the papers. We needed a name, and I like the sound of that one. Would you ladies like to sit?" He asked because he was obviously ready to enjoy his breakfast but wished to be a gentleman.

George took a seat at the far end of the table, the lift of her brow a sign that she found this conversation quite entertaining.

Celeste shook her head. She wasn't ready to sit. "But that *isn't* the name of the charity."

Having done his gentlemanly duty, Salcombe took his chair. "It must be now. It is in all the morning papers. It will be in the evening ones as well." He drained the tankard of ale. "That *is* good. Your man says you brew it yourselves."

"Yes, we do," Celeste said absently, her mind roiling with his impertinence. He had renamed *her* charity, and without a word to her. She had wanted to call it Heroes of the War. Our Brave Soldiers was not terrible... but it wasn't her idea. "You do remember that my late father tasked *me* with establishing a charity?"

"I do." He picked up a knife and fork and plunged into his food.

Celeste drew in a deep breath and decided the duke's choice of name was not so bad. "Very well. Our Brave Soldiers. And you have already sent out notices to the papers?"

"My man Peters took care of the matter yesterday."

He'd known he was going to help her *yesterday*? But he had not thought to say one word to her?

"Oh," was all Celeste could think to reply without losing her temper and shouting. She had toyed with the wording of several notices for the newspapers but had, of course, been waiting until she had acquired a lead patron. "Well," she managed, "another task done."

"We will hold a subscription ball," the duke informed her as if she'd asked. "I shall host it. I don't often entertain at Salcombe House. Peters and the staff are excited about this endeavor. He has made a guest list that includes everyone of importance. We should do very well."

A subscription ball was a must. It was the way most charities funded themselves. Celeste had been concerned that, since the London house was her mother's territory, a ball might be difficult to accomplish. Her mother could be very particular. She was also a friend of Lady Redhill's. If Lady Redhill disapproved, her mother would have rejected

Celeste's request. So, the offer of his hospitality was indeed appreciated, although Celeste thought it would have been nice if he even pretended to consult her wishes.

From the other end of the table, George smiled, the expression that of a cat who drank the cream. She knew exactly what Celeste was thinking, especially as the duke went on about *his* ideas and *his* plans and *his* thoughts.

The longer he talked, the more Celeste felt a strong desire to take one of the silver domed covers on the dishes and clang him over the head with it.

Finally, finished with his meal and soliloquy, Salcombe wiped his mouth with a napkin and stood, assuring her, "We will be the talk of the Town."

"You mean, *my* charity will be the talk of the Town."

"Of course." He strode out into the hall, and Celeste hopped up and hurried to follow him out. George trailed behind them at a more leisurely pace.

"Tell your brewer he is an artist," the duke said. "I enjoy a hoppy ale."

"I shall pass that on," Celeste replied tightly.

"Oh," he said as he took his hat from the footman. "Will you be at the Deveraux affair tomorrow?"

"We were not sent an invitation." Lord Deveraux and his wife fancied themselves the cream of society and enjoyed wielding their high opinion of themselves like a cudgel. They liked letting people know through their invitations when they did not meet their inflated standards.

"I'll change that. You need to be seen so you can answer questions about Our Brave Soldiers." He grinned. "We will need to think about what to do with the men once they are off the streets. I already have our first soldier. You were right about their companion animals. His is a mixed-breed, little hellion named Pistol. We will have to move them soon because Pistol has been chasing the stable cats. My grooms are annoyed. Apparently, they considered those cats to be *their* pets." He shook his head as if he didn't understand their attitude at all. Then, with a final nod, he was out the front door.

Celeste watched him mount his horse and trot off without so much as a backward wave—and then she allowed the full weight of his call sink in. He'd *known* he was going to support her yesterday . . . but couldn't be bothered to say anything? Not even pen a quick note?

And then her twin spoke. "It seems, Cece, you have caught a Dragon by the tail." George was barely able to contain her mirth.

Celeste's answer was to march off to the garden, her heels clicking on the wood floor. She took five turns around the various flower beds before she could think reasonably. She should be happy. The charity would be a success—that is, if she didn't murder Salcombe first.

And that was becoming a *very* big "if."

An hour later, a servant knocked on their door with an invitation to the Deveraux affair for not only all of the Harrington sisters and their mother—who had dearly wished for an invite—but for Dame Beatrice as well.

Because, apparently, the Duke of Salcombe had thought of everything.

6

From the moment the announcement about Our Brave Soldiers appeared in the papers, all credit for the idea was given to the Duke of Salcombe.

Everyone, from the most prestigious of nobles down to chimney sweeps and ratcatchers, believed a charity for soldiers who had lost limbs, and therefore their livelihoods, while fighting for their country, was an excellent idea. They knew the government pensions weren't enough and never would be to support these former soldiers. Salcombe was lauded for his foresight, patriotism, and generosity.

And Celeste was pleased that it appeared her charity would be a success—except, being ignored when it had been *her* idea originally stung.

To his credit, the duke tried to include Celeste. He ensured Celeste and her family, as well as Dame Beatrice, were invited to every rout, ball, and event he attended. When hosts and hostesses drew him up on a dais to speak to the gathering about Our Brave Soldiers, he asked Celeste to stand by his side. When questions were asked, he deferred them to her.

But that didn't mean she was given any credit.

The world insisted he be in charge. Everyone acted drawn to this new, responsible Duke of Salcombe. Even Lord Liverpool sought him out for conversations. Celeste couldn't help but feel abandoned.

Especially since Salcombe had been all that was proper after that one, singular kiss. It was almost as if he didn't recall the kiss. What had been a revelation for her had apparently not been all that interesting to him.

But he did call often and seemed to enjoy teasing her. A time or two, he would touch her. It was not anything dramatic—a brush on her arm, perhaps leaning a touch closer than one should, that sort of thing. One day, when he was driving her around the park so she could privately school him on what he should say at an upcoming meeting at his club, he pulled over.

"Is something the matter?" she asked.

"The wind," he answered and then, removing one glove, gently tucked one of her curls that had blown free from under her bonnet back behind her ear.

His expression was intent, as if he was concentrating on the task, wanting to see it done right. His face was mere inches from hers. His eyes lifted to meet hers. Their gazes held.

She found it hard to breathe, let alone think.

Then he sat back, smiled at her, put on his glove, and they were off again… as if nothing untoward had taken place.

George believed he didn't have to call on them as often as he did. "He is interested in you," she said.

"Nonsense. He can have any woman he wants." Why should he settle on her? There were many women more statuesque, more beautiful.

"Then why is he here every time we turn around?"

"He likes our chef and our brewer."

"I think he likes *you*," George insisted.

Those were dangerous words. Celeste mulled over them more than she should. Occasionally, she sensed him watching her. Except when she looked in his direction, his attention was always on something or someone else. Never her. She needed to keep herself in check.

Furthermore, he was high-handed and male—and therein lay the challenge.

CELESTE WAS DRESSED but had not yet had a cup of strong tea or a bite of toast when Rodman knocked on her bedroom door and informed her that Salcombe was currently sitting at their breakfast table, *again*.

George was still abed but overheard. "I'll be down to chaperone," her twin groaned and stretched her arms. "Provided I can manage to open my eyes. The fireworks at the Lovetts' were spectacular. A pity you and Josephine had already gone home." She referred to their youngest sister.

Celeste and Josephine had left the ball shortly after Salcombe took his leave. He'd taken a moment to address Lord Fromhurst, who had requested to speak to him alone about the charity. They all wanted to speak to him. Alone. She was never invited into those conversations. She supposed that the duke and Lord Fromhurst had gone off to one of London's gentlemen's clubs. Women were not invited.

And here was the galling thing: After his departure, Celeste discovered that the ball had gone decidedly flat.

Now, he was downstairs...waiting for her. He might have information about his discussion with Lord Fromhurst.

"You sleep," she advised George. "He's here so often, no one will bat an eye about my meeting him over breakfast. He does like Cook's beefsteak."

"He likes *you*," George answered.

Celeste kept her opinion to herself. There was no arguing with George.

In the family dining room, she found Salcombe happily drinking Kenbrooks ale and munching on a mound of bacon. Without any greeting, he said, "Fromhurst wants to be a named patron—"

"A patron?" She frowned down at him seated at the table.

"—I told him yes. I will also be meeting with the Marquess of Penaly in an hour. He's a morning person as well. He wants to be a patron of the charity, too."

Celeste stared at him. "Wait. How many patrons will we have?"

"As many as wish to pay," he assured her.

"How many have *you* agreed to?"

He lifted his eyes to the ceiling as if mentally counting and then shrugged. "I'm not certain."

She wanted to growl her frustration. "We must keep track," she said, struggling to keep her tone civil. "We can't have half of London listed as patrons."

"I can for our charity," he explained as if it were obvious.

He'd said *our*. She registered the word.

Except he'd also said "I." *I can for our charity.*

Her temper ignited.

He was *always* making decisions without a word to her. Just as he'd changed the name of the charity. Just as he'd been going around London inviting dispossessed soldiers to join them—something she couldn't do because single women of a certain class couldn't approach men on the street without being misunderstood as to their intentions. Just as he was obviously making promises in meetings she could not attend.

It was not right. Why were men free to do whatever they wished? No one suspected their motives or branded them as too forward. Men also expected the world to bow to their demands while they ignored the women with ideas—

"*My* charity." The words flew out of her. "This is *my* idea."

"True," he answered. He nabbed a soft, hot bun off the plate and talked around bites. "But I am your lead patron."

"Apparently, you are one of what's becoming a legion of patrons. However, *I'm* the one who makes *decisions*." There, she'd said it. She had laid down the law. And it had taken all of her courage, all of her energy.

He hooked an arm on the back of his chair, completely at ease with himself. He enjoyed taking up all the space in the room, she thought peevishly. "You are upset," he observed.

"You noticed, Your Grace."

He pressed his lips together, thought a moment, and seemed to come to a decision. Sounding somewhat contrite, he said, "I fear what you will consider a truly major decision may have been made without you."

Her back straightened. "What have you done?"

Salcombe glanced at her cooling tea. "You might wish to sit and take a sip of your brew before we discuss this."

"Answer my question."

A footman entered the room with her toast. He set it before her.

The duke said, "Enjoy your breakfast, my lady. We can discuss this later—"

"*What* decision?

He released a soft sigh, his brows rising as if in regret. "Well, I may have agreed to purchase a property. One where the men could live...along with their pets."

For a second, Celeste didn't believe she had heard him correctly. "Purchased a property?" she repeated, ignoring his soft jibe about pets. He had been hoping to deflect her attention from what he'd just admitted. "I saw you last evening. Had you purchased the property by then?"

"No." He took a drag of his ale, his gaze moving away from hers. "And I still haven't purchased it. Not until I see it. But the deal is fairly well done."

"*How* did you make an agreement between last night and now? It is half past eight in the morning. Or did you do this at midnight? And why are you leaving me, *the owner of the charity,* out of the discussion?"

The footman shot a nervous glance at her. She frowned. "Please give us privacy, Stephen." With a curt bow, the servant made a hasty retreat from the room.

Seemingly unperturbed, His Grace leaned over and plucked a piece of toast from her toast rack. He chomped down on half of it before saying, "It was around midnight when I talked to Masick. I came across him at Fromhurst's club. Masick's land borders my estate in Greenwich. He has been yapping at me for months to take it off his hands. He gambles. Poorly, I might add."

He paused as if expecting her to reply. She didn't say a word. She didn't trust herself to speak. Her nails bit into the palms of her clenched fists. The effort of restraining herself was mighty, and he must have sensed it. "I do wish you would sit—"

"I'm *fine*."

The duke eyed her as if he didn't agree, but he wisely didn't contradict her. Instead, he spread his hands as if to show he meant no tricks. "I haven't decided on the property yet. I'm going to Greenwich to look over the land tomorrow and see if it meets our needs—"

Celeste could contain herself no longer. "*My* needs. *My* charity. *My* idea. I'm honoring a request from *my* late father." She faced Salcombe, so angry she didn't know what she would do next. "You have taken a great deal upon yourself."

"You told me you wanted a place in the country for the men to live...with their pets. I'm attempting to help, Celeste."

He'd used her given name. A day ago, she might have been flattered. Right now, she was annoyed. "Not by cutting me out of important decisions, *Oliver*."

Her return use of his name made him sit up. The steel in his eyes met the steel she knew was in hers, but she would not back down. There would be no simpering from her, not on a matter of such importance. Her father had given her this task and she would be in charge.

She knew he didn't understand her feelings. Why would he? He had all the advantages. Meanwhile, she had been pushed to the side, and she hated that all the world would believe he was correct to do as he wished.

The duke backed down first. "I've upset you, and that wasn't my purpose. It was not my choice to leave you out of meeting with Masick. But Fromhurst and I met at his club, at his request," he hastened to add.

"You could have suggested a meeting place where I might attend."

"Not at that hour of night."

He was right. No, it wasn't his fault. Or, at least, not his fault alone. She also needed to remember that her charity had only been a dream until he became involved.

Still, that didn't make being refused a role in important discussions easier. "You and Lord Penaly will meet at a club, even though it is morning?" she said tightly.

"Yes." He paused and then said, "It is where men gather, my lady. There is no insult intended. However, I came here to keep you informed because it is *your* charity."

He sounded sincere, but she was overwhelmed by the unfairness of it all. "Everyone thinks you are wonderful."

"I take pains to give you full credit, my lady."

"You do." At last, she sat, momentarily defeated. Her tea was cold and her toast half eaten. A new idea formed. "I want to see the property."

"It would be my honor to give you a tour of it."

"You will not buy that property until I have seen it."

"I'm walking it tomorrow. Masick is desperate and will give us a good price if I give him an answer immediately."

"Then I'll go with you tomorrow."

He contemplated her a moment before saying carefully, "Greenwich is a day's drive from here."

She tilted her head, her suspicions rising. "Are you saying you don't want me to go?"

He held up his hand as if to ward off any accusations. "I would be honored to have you as my guest at Elberling. That is my estate next to Masick's land."

She nodded, slightly mollified. "Thank you. I accept your invitation."

He nodded and shifted in his chair as if relieved he had avoided another salvo from her. "Do you still wish me to see Penaly this morning?"

"Yes," she conceded. "Because we will need his and all the other new patrons' money to purchase the land."

"I can purchase the land, my lady."

It was a generous offer, one that spoke of his commitment to the charity...something, she realized she had rudely ignored.

The duke had also not referred to her by her given name after her flash of temper. He might not ever do so again. She had been wrong to lash out. It had not been well-mannered. But she would not apologize. She had needed to speak up for herself.

She also realized that she had placed her hand on the table in entreaty and let it rest there. His hand was also there, his fingers a mere inch from hers. She stared at his long, strong fingers. A swordsman's hand. A capable hand.

Silence unspooled around them. She raised her gaze to find him watching her. Outside the room, household sounds drifted down the hall as the world stirred. But in this room, there was the deep quiet of something unspoken. She wished she could divine what he was thinking. He was not a simple man. He was more intelligent and altruistic than society knew. And respect was a gift that ran both ways.

She spoke. "I appreciate your offer, Your Grace. I cannot buy the property— not yet, at least. Once the charity is set up, I will come into an inheritance."

"An inheritance?"

"Yes, it is the terms of Father's will. He's giving each of my sisters and me a task. Once it is finished, we receive a gift of money. I intend to use my money for the charity. It doesn't seem right to keep it for myself when others are in so much need."

Something seemed to ease inside of him as if he was coming to a decision. He stood slowly.

She frowned. She wasn't ready for him to leave.

He said, "I'll send my coach for you in the morning. Half past ten? Is that good?"

Celeste couldn't stop her smile. She was going to Greenwich with him. "Yes, Your Grace."

He scowled. "Stop the formalities. You just called me Oliver. Please continue. I give you leave. We are in this endeavor together. Hopefully, one of these days you will trust me?"

She thought of his hand so close to hers a mere minute before. "I do trust you."

"You are a poor liar, Celeste."

That was true. She ducked her head so he couldn't see how ridiculously pleased she was that he had used her given name again.

"You will need a chaperone—and don't spout nonsense about being seven and twenty," he warned as he started for the door. "I'll not be your ruin."

"Have the coach pick me up at Dame Beatrice's residence, then." Celeste wasn't about to ask her mother or one of her sisters to accompany her. This was her adventure. Her way of honoring her late father's memory . . . and her opportunity to feel an equal to the duke. She surprised herself at how important that was to her. Bea wouldn't distract or judge her like her family would. "I'll write the address." She hurried down the hall to her brother's study. Scratching out the address, she left the room to find the duke waiting for her in the front hall.

She handed him the slip of paper. "Thank you," she said.

He tipped his hat and left.

The moment the door shut, Celeste almost crumpled with exhaustion. Standing up for oneself was trying business... especially against him. Everything about Oliver challenged her. He was too bold, too quick...too handsome.

Oh, yes, she was more than attracted to him.

She needed to remember he wasn't interested in her. Not

truly. He was a rake. Rakes knew how to tap into women's senses, into their emotions. It was their nature. He couldn't help but lure her to him.

Except, she was stronger than most women, she told herself... and prayed that was true as she headed up the stairs to tell George a story about Dame Beatrice inviting her for a visit.

OLIVER EXPERTLY STEERED his high-perch phaeton around a couple crossing the road as he drove away. Lady Celeste—*Celeste*, he liked her name, and he liked that she pushed back against him.

Because he liked *her*.

True, she was a guarded creature. She didn't trust easily, but neither did he.

She'd also changed his life. Because of her, his peers now considered him a leader, a man of substance.

Celeste had done that. Celeste had created the opportunity that led others to see him for who he was.

However, something else was going on.

He wasn't a dullard. He knew when a woman was attracted to him. However, he couldn't remember the last time that he'd felt the same in return. Her approval was important to him. When he was with her, he felt purposeful, and he liked her speaking to him as an equal.

And when her eyes lit up with indignation, when she challenged him, when she spoke her mind, he found her magnificent.

7

Oliver didn't visit the Elberling estate often. It had never been a favorite of his family. So, he was apprehensive about the state of the house, especially since he barely remembered the place. He had grown up in the family home in Dartmoor.

"It is a different home when compared to the usual country manor," he warned Dame Beatrice and Celeste.

"We shall judge for ourselves," Celeste answered and suggested they play cards to pass the time. Dame Beatrice said she preferred to nap and promptly fell asleep.

Oliver was not unhappy having Celeste to himself. Nor was he surprised when she expected him to be a worthy opponent. She was, also, an intelligent card player. The conversation between them was easy, and the day was a good one for travel. The breeze was pleasant, the road smooth, and his new coach remarkably well-sprung.

Of course, traveling and riding side-by-side in even a fine coach like this meant that they would brush up against each other. His legs took up the most space, but Celeste did not complain, even when their knees bumped. Her delicate fragrance of cherry and rose seemed to swirl around him. He thought of asking what perfume she favored but feared she would think him overly familiar.

"What is the plan for tomorrow?" she asked him, placing her cards down on the travel table they were using.

"The ride to Masick's land will take an hour."

"That long?"

"Elberling is a rather large estate." Although not the largest of his holdings. "I imagine it will take us a few hours to tour the property Masick has for sale."

She stifled a yawn and smiled at him. "It isn't the company."

"I hope not," he said and shuffled the cards for another game.

Sooner than he wished, they turned into the drive leading to Elberling. The coach's change of speed roused Dame Beatrice. She sat up, blinking. "Your Grace, this is a remarkable conveyance."

"I am pleased you are enjoying it, my lady."

"I should say I am. I haven't slept that deeply in ages. I may have to take a turn every afternoon in this vehicle while we are here."

"I shall see it is at your disposal, my lady."

Dame Beatrice smiled. "You are a charmer, Your Grace."

He hoped everyone in the coach felt that way. However, Celeste didn't appear to be paying attention. She looked out the window as if anxious to arrive, and then she sucked in her breath as if surprised. "The house!" She turned to Oliver. "Was it an abbey?"

"Centuries ago."

"It is magical."

Magical. Oliver had never applied that word to anything in his life. Certainly not to Elberling's crumbling walls that served as a testament to the building's once holy past.

However, as he looked out the coach window, a change fell over him. Yes, the arches of the abbey's once proud walls were almost in ruins, but enough remained intact to show how majestic they had once been.

Behind the walls was the old stone building that had been built centuries ago. He had stewards to take care of each of his estates. His man here was obviously doing an excellent job. The late afternoon light hit the walls at just the right angle, giving the hard lines of the gray stone a silvery glaze.

"Those trees appear to have been planted the year the abbey was built," Celeste said about the huge oaks with their spreading branches. "They have seen stories."

He remembered the trees. He'd climbed them as a lad but he'd never considered their lifespan or the history they had witnessed. *His* history. The stories of those trees involved his ancestors. There were a few unsavory tales. His great-grandfathers had often taken what they wanted. Succeeding dukes, like himself, preferred London. However, as he watched Celeste, her eyes sparkling as she admired the home *he* took for granted, he realized magic *was* entering his life. And it had started the moment she'd sent him the note that led to their meeting in the library.

"I suppose it is very drafty," Dame Beatrice said.

"All of Britain is, Bea," Celeste replied. "That is why I knitted woolen socks for your birthday."

"True," the dame allowed, and then her gaze fell on Oliver. Her brows lifted. Had what he'd been thinking shown on his face?

Her expression softened, and he realized he had an ally.

The coach traveled under the arches and around to the

front door of the stone building. "I'm so ready to be out of this confined space," Celeste said.

When his coachman opened the door, she was the first to hop out. She waited impatiently for Oliver. "You must give us a tour this very moment."

"Happily, once you have seen your rooms and had a moment to yourselves," he said, playing the host.

While the housekeeper, Mrs. Hillsdale, took the women down the hallway to the guest quarters, Oliver stayed in the reception hall, where refreshments had been laid out for the travelers.

To his surprise, Dame Beatrice joined him first. He poured her a sherry.

Taking the glass from him, she said, "I don't disapprove of you, Your Grace, despite you being too handsome for your own good."

"Is that a compliment?"

"That you aren't the blackguard some believe? Absolutely. But I also sense that you are more than fond of Celeste?"

He noted the question in her tone. "I admire her greatly."

"I think she admires you as well."

"She does?" He'd wanted this confirmation.

"Do not be too pleased with yourself, Your Grace. I plan on being a dutiful chaperone."

He thought of her snoring on the coach ride, and yet, he could see her becoming as fierce as a tiger if she decided Celeste needed protecting.

Before he could answer, she turned to the hallway door with a smile. "Celeste dear, come see this delicious tray of sweet breads the duke's staff has prepared."

"I don't wish to spoil my supper," Celeste replied,

approaching them. She didn't take the sherry Oliver offered but chose a glass of sweet cider instead. "And now, Your Grace, you owe me a tour. Will you join us, my lady?"

"I shall stay here with the sherry," Dame Beatrice said and reached for another sweet bread. "You can tell me all about it later."

Celeste turned to the duke expectantly. He offered his arm. For the next hour, he took her from room to room. She seemed to have a hundred questions in each room, and Oliver could barely answer one. Fortunately, Avery, the butler, lingered in the hallway, ready to offer assistance when Oliver turned to him.

"You don't seem as if you know this house very well," she said, when Avery excused himself to see how dinner was progressing.

"I don't," he admitted. "I haven't been here since I was a child."

"Why is that?"

"My mother liked it, so Father didn't wish to visit often because they didn't seem to rub along well. I was happier spending most of my time at school."

"My parents didn't like each other either. Although they had nine children together."

"Are you one who believes marriage is about duty?" He didn't know why he'd asked such a question, and yet, once spoken, he was curious about her answer.

"Like the marriages our parents obviously had? It seems the happiest people are in relationships based on love. And I do believe love should be valued."

"Because you are a romantic?"

"Because I believe we should surround ourselves with people and things we love. I enjoying being close to my brother and sisters. They matter to me even when I find them annoying. However, when it comes to a place to live, if I were you, *this* would be my home. I like the peace of it. Of course, I would make improvements. Some of these rooms need new furnishings—oh, wait, is that a dog?" She was looking toward the hall.

Dog? There were no dogs here, and then Oliver saw a black shadow cross the door.

"A *dog*," she repeated happily, moving toward the door. "Come here, come here," she called softly.

Sure enough, a black terrier peeked his head through the door as if to question whether she was talking to him. He was solid black with a shiny nose and laughing eyes as if he knew his own worth. Celeste made a delighted sound. "A Scottish terrier."

Just as she reached to give the dog a pat, Mrs. Hillsdale came racing through the doorway. She swept the dog into her arms. "I'm so sorry, Your Grace. Muggins snuck into the house."

"He is your dog?" Celeste placed her hand gently on Muggins's panting head. "He is such a handsome laddie."

"Muggins is a handful is what he is," Mrs. Hillsdale replied. "He shouldn't be in the house." There was a somewhat staged tone to her comment.

"All dogs belong in the house," Celeste assured her. "I enjoy my pets at Fenmere Park. That is our country estate. Dogs, cats, why, I'd let the horse inside if they would allow me." She looked up at Oliver. "Let Muggins stay? I miss my dogs."

His mother would never have allowed an animal in the house. Dogs belonged in the stables, according to her. Except, looking into Celeste's pleading eyes and knowing her affinity for "pets," Oliver knew she would not be happy if he banned Muggins from the house.

And in that moment, he knew that he wanted to keep Celeste happy.

It made him feel good to say, "Of course, he can remain inside—provided he stays away from my boots."

Mrs. Hillsdale's face lit with delight. "Thank you, Your Grace. He will behave. He is not a chewer, well, not much of one."

Oliver didn't believe that. Muggins appeared as if he did whatever he pleased.

However, Celeste beamed at him, and Oliver felt noble in a way he could never have previously imagined.

At that moment, Avery announced dinner.

Celeste and Oliver returned to the reception hall to gather Dame Beatrice, and they had a companionable, delicious dinner. Someplace between the cheese and the pudding, he realized that the loneliness that had so often troubled him had vanished.

He had hoped to spend more time alone with Celeste after the meal, but when Dame Beatrice declared herself ready for bed, Celeste agreed that she was tired as well.

Oliver escorted the two women to their rooms. If he thought Celeste might linger, he was disappointed.

"We have a big day tomorrow," she said. "Good night—" She paused and then tacked on, "Oliver."

"Good night, Celeste." The door shut quietly.

He stood a moment, staring at the polished wood. *Magic*. She'd used the word earlier to describe Elberling, but he thought it better described Celeste, with her remarkable eyes and heavenly scent, and her generous nature.

Oliver took a step back, and then another, though the last thing he wanted was to walk away from her.

So, he went to his room. Alone.

Well, not completely alone. His sheets had been turned

down. A lamp burned on the bedside table. And Muggins lay on his back in the middle of the coverlet. He appeared completely at his ease.

A manservant, who was acting as his valet, came walking in behind Oliver, carrying a pitcher of steaming water and some linen towels. "I'm sorry, Your Grace. I meant to have this ready before you—" The servant stopped short. "*Muggins.* Down from there." The manservant set the pitcher on the wash basin before racing to the bed. "I am so sorry, Your Grace. So sorry. Muggins, *down*."

Muggins did not move. It was as if he owned the bed.

The servant would have grabbed the dog and carried him out, but Oliver stayed him with one hand. "What is your name?"

The man swallowed as if he feared he was in trouble. "Henry, Your Grace."

"Thank you for the water, Henry. I can see myself to bed. And don't worry about Muggins. He appears quite comfortable."

"He will catch it when Mrs. Hillsdale learns where he is."

"Then we won't tell her. Good night, Henry."

The servant could barely hide his surprise, but Muggins began panting as if he was laughing. Unlike the family hunting hounds, the terrier seemed to understand humans.

Oliver climbed into bed. He was amused to hear the dog grumble as he sullenly made room for Oliver's much larger body. Muggins curled up beside him, his back to Oliver, and both man and beast fell asleep.

8

Celeste woke up confused. She had been attracted to the duke, to his reputation, and even to his arrogance. However, she was seeing a different side to him, a human one. If he'd been as arrogant as he seemed in London, she could ignore her attraction to him. Instead, here in the country, he'd deferred to his butler and had acted a bit sheepish that he hadn't known more about his own house.

One of his own houses, she reminded herself.

"I do find I like him," she whispered to the ceiling. But he could do better than her. She had no doubt every heiress in London chased him. "I'm not going to lose my head over him." It was a promise to herself, one she intended to keep because nothing was worse than pining for what she couldn't have.

She put a leg over the edge of the bed. "My charity," she said aloud. "*Mine.*" But her declaration sounded hollow. She wouldn't have reached the point of buying property or even holding a ball for subscribers without Oliver.

And while Celeste wished she had more control over the

planning of the ball, she could admit that Mr. Peters, the duke's man, was better organized than she could ever have been. So, perhaps she should stop being defensive. She was the one who had begged for Oliver's help.

Less than an hour later, she was dressed for riding and on her way down to the breakfast room. She heard voices and entered the room to see Beatrice and the duke at the table together. Beatrice was laughing and sought to cover her mouth with her napkin.

To Celeste's surprise, Muggins sat on his haunches on the duke's lap. Right there at the table.

"What is so funny?" Celeste asked.

"Watch," Beatrice ordered as the duke tore off a bit of the bacon on his plate and offered it to the dog.

Instead of being docile and grateful, Muggins ducked under Salcombe's arm and stole the larger piece of the meat, gobbling it fast.

"He's a rascal," Oliver said, rubbing the dog's ear with affection.

At that moment, Mrs. Hillsdale came to a halt in the doorway, staring at the dog. "I have been looking all over for him. I beg your pardon, Your Grace. He should be outside where he belongs. Come now, Mister." She went to reach for the pup, but Salcombe stopped her with a frown.

"I have been told by one and all that Muggins spends most of his time in the house."

Mrs. Hillsdale dropped her hands, her expression stricken. She glanced at the footman by the door who ducked his head. Turning back to the duke, she replied, "He will not in the future. I must also confess I lost him last night. I spent a good amount of time looking for him. However, I fear he is a bit of a weasel when it comes to having his way."

"He was with me," the duke said, "And please do not worry. Muggins is welcome in the house, *provided* he stays away from my boots," he said, reiterating the warning he'd given the day before. However, this time, he directed his comment to the dog who acted unconcerned.

"He will, Your Grace. I promise he will." The housekeeper picked up Muggins.

"Actually, Mrs. Hillsdale, he is a fine character. I imagine Muggins rules the place when I am not here."

"Mr. Avery likes him, so he does let him do whatever he pleases," she replied.

"Ah, yes, I am certain it is Avery who has spoiled him."

"I certainly do not," she answered, but she was smiling. Celeste noticed the footman seemed relieved that all would be well. Muggins was obviously a favorite in the household among the staff.

After the dog had been carried away, Celeste helped herself to the dishes on the sideboard. "Has Muggins made a dog lover of you, Your Grace?"

"I like Muggins more than most of the members of Parliament." He set his napkin aside. "Are you ready to view the Masick property, my lady?"

Celeste hopped to her feet, picking up the bun from her plate that she hadn't finished eating. "We'll see you later, Beatrice."

The duke had arranged a lovely bay mare for Celeste to ride. The animal was well-trained with a gentle temperament. He rode his beast of a horse, Johnny.

Again, conversation flowed easily between them. They talked about everything from events of the day to books they'd enjoyed to plans for the charity as they cut across the plowed fields. Oliver knew the way, and she was happy to follow. She enjoyed being on the back of a good horse again.

"I have been thinking about what rules we should have for the men living on the property," she said.

"What have you decided?"

"That most of the rules should be determined by the men themselves. After all, they were all soldiers once. They know how to keep good order."

He nodded his agreement. "I also accept how important their dogs may be to them. However, you mentioned cats. I don't know about cats. Cats don't strike me as loyal to anyone."

"They can be very companionable," Celeste assured him. "When I was a girl, I had an orange tabby named Mortimer who followed me everywhere. He'd even let me dress him up in a doll bonnet. He could open closed doors. He'd jump up, catch the latch, and pull down on it. I also adore seeing a cat napping in the window seat of a room."

Oliver made a face. "I'll wait to be convinced."

She laughed. "All we need is a cat with a personality as big as the one Muggins has."

"That would be hard to find," he assured her, and she promised him that, someday, he'd meet a cat who would change his mind. She knew it wouldn't be hard. She was quickly learning that Oliver had a big heart. It was becoming what she admired the most about him.

They were met at the appointed place by a Mr. Vickery, Lord Masick's land agent, who gave them the tour. There was a house, but it needed work. Celeste was a bit dismayed by how much would need to be repaired.

However, Oliver assured her the pensioners would be happy to see to the repairs. "The barn and stables are in good shape," he pointed out.

She agreed. "What of families, though? The men should be able to start families."

"They can build the cottages themselves. The charity will provide the materials."

Celeste liked the idea, especially after Mr. Vickery showed them a level pasture that would make it easy to create a village of cottages. By the end of the tour, she was impressed with the property and grateful to Oliver for having found it.

"Are you hungry?" he asked.

"Famished."

"The Forest Hare is down the road a bit," Mr. Vickery offered helpfully. They said their goodbyes and rode to the public house that wasn't far from the main road.

The duke ordered ale and a steak while Celeste chose a roasted chicken and some cider. After the serving woman left them, she assumed they would continue to discuss their plans for the pensioners.

Instead, Salcombe surprised her by asking, "Am I forgiven for naming the charity Our Brave Soldiers without your approval?"

She blushed, slightly embarrassed by how angry she'd been. "You have made up for the transgression. And it is a good title."

"But have I regained your trust?"

He was serious, she realized. He sounded as if her answer mattered to him.

She warned herself to be careful, to not read too much into the question. Keeping her tone light, she said, "I thought dukes, especially one considered to be a dragon, didn't worry about what people thought of them."

"I'm not asking 'people.' I'm asking *you*. I know I can be domineering. However, this charity means a great deal to me. I don't wish to live a shallow life. I also feel an affinity for those men. All any of us desire is an opportunity to be treated with respect. I believe we will give that to a good number of men who deserve it."

"It is the purpose of this whole endeavor," she agreed. Her father would have been proud.

"So, I ask again, am I forgiven?"

"There is nothing to forgive, Oliver. You were acting as you thought best."

The corner of his mouth quirked to one side, and then he said, "I remember you reacted with strong feelings." He paused and then added, "However, I have tried to earn your trust."

"Does it matter, Your Grace?" she asked.

"It matters to me, Celeste."

He sounded sincere. She could feel him watching her closely. And suddenly, the air between them seemed thick with unspoken questions, questions she would *never* ask.

Deep within her, she could hear George's voice saying *he's interested in you.*

She took in his features, the intensity in his eyes, the lines of his nobly handsome face, the broad shoulders, the man who could have any woman he wanted. Why would he settle for her?

In that moment, she felt vulnerable. She didn't like the feeling. For the briefest second, her heart urged her to risk all and confess that not only did she trust him, but she also admired him—no, that wasn't the truth. She was falling in love with him.

Of course, she was just one of a legion of women who yearned for Oliver. And she needed to remember that. Her pride demanded it.

She stood. "We should be leaving." She didn't wait for him but marched for the door. He had no choice but to stay behind and pay for their meal. She waited outside, taking deep breaths and having a stern, silent lecture with herself. She had no desire to appear a fool.

He joined her. "Celeste—" he started, but she interrupted.

"The groom has fetched the horses," she said brightly, as if all was fine. "Look, here he is." She didn't wait for his help to mount but let the groom assist her. Soon they were on their way back to Elberling.

She spoke first, returning the conversation to safe topics, like the charity, or the weather, or what a sweet mount she was riding. He answered politely, but she sensed his annoyance, and the earlier ease between them had vanished.

They were in sight of Elberling's arched walls when he suddenly reached for her rein and pulled her mare to a stop. Celeste frowned. "What is the matter?"

"You ask me what is the matter? You have been chattering without pause ever since the inn."

"I thought I was making conversation," she replied, her heart in her throat.

"You were putting me off." He let go of the rein. "The one thing I've always counted on with you, Celeste, is your honesty. Your directness. However, something is bothering you, and don't push me away with more talk about the weather. Your eyes give away everything you are thinking. You became upset when I asked if you trusted me. What is it, Celeste? What have I done?"

You let me fall in love with you. She kept that thought to herself. Instead, she met his eye with what she hoped was a neutral expression and said, "Nothing is wrong. I trust you."

The lines of his face hardened with disappointment.

"I do," she pressed. "I trust you."

Without a word, he turned his horse toward the house. Celeste watched him ride away. The man was maddening.

She had the right to keep her thoughts to herself. And besides, who cared if she trusted him or not? She was surprised that he did...and then alarmed that their relationship, something she valued, was in danger of being destroyed.

She kicked her horse forward. Once she was alongside him again, she said, "Why are you acting this way?"

"What way, Celeste?"

"As if I—" She paused, searching for the right words, words that didn't reveal her own fears, doubts, and desires. "As if I have disappointed you."

They had reached the front steps. Grooms ran forward to take their horses. This was not the time for an argument, and yet, Celeste didn't want these sour feelings to remain between them.

She waited until she had dismounted, expecting him to wait for her. Instead, in a breach of manners, he was already moving toward the front door. She hurried to catch him. He had to know she was behind him. She followed him into the house. "Your Grace," she dared to say, conscious of the servants around them.

Muggins came charging forward to greet the duke, his nails scrabbling on the wood floor. He bent down to give the dog a scratch behind the ears. Celeste used this moment to say in the lowest voice possible, "I do trust you."

Oliver straightened. He handed his hat and riding gloves to a footman before turning to her and saying, "Then be honest with me."

"I am."

His somber eyes met hers. They narrowed slightly, and then, without a word to her, he went up the stairs, Muggins following happily at his heels.

9

"How was the property?" Beatrice asked when Celeste came down after changing for dinner. Bea was in the receiving room enjoying more of Salcombe's sherry.

"Good," Celeste answered.

"Would you care for a drink?" Bea asked. "It is very good sherry."

Celeste shook her head.

Her friend frowned. "What is the matter?"

But before Celeste could answer, Oliver joined them. A subdued Oliver. Oh, he was amiable enough but quiet, and he didn't look at her. Once they sat down for dinner, Bea asked him about the property, and he expounded as little as Celeste had. Her friend looked from him to Celeste, who concentrated on buttering a slice of bread.

Celeste was quickly understanding that his pique, as she was beginning to think of it, was all for the better. He was keeping his distance, and that was the way things should be.

Bea acted puzzled but carried on. She smiled as if she didn't notice anything amiss—until they left the table and adjourned to the sitting room. There, Oliver made his apologies and excused himself for the evening.

Once they were alone, Bea didn't waste a moment. "What is going on? Did you and the duke have words?"

"Not really. Everything was fine until it wasn't."

"Tell me everything." And so, to her surprise, Celeste did. She wasn't one to blurt out her feelings on something so personal, even to Bea. However, this was a moment when she needed to confide in someone.

When she was done, Beatrice said, "This confirms my suspicions."

"And what do you think?"

"That he is interested in you. Certainly, he wants you. He stares at you whenever he thinks you aren't looking. Even this evening."

"I didn't notice." She'd been too uncomfortable.

"Celeste, he hangs on your every word. He listens to you."

"He is dedicated to the charity—" Celeste started.

"He wants *you*." Beatrice's words echoed George's claim.

The idea was still too fantastical for Celeste to believe. "The Dragon of London can't be interested in me."

"Whyever not?"

"I'm a bit—" She searched for the right word. "Pugnacious, to be honest. I've also been called too independent. And there are women who are far better looking than I am who have tried and failed to capture his attention."

"Maybe, he has come to recognize your value. You are lovely, Celeste, even though you aren't what is in fashion. Few of us are. However, a man worthy of you will appreciate what you bring to his life. I find Salcombe a true gentleman, regardless of what the gossips say. The question is, what do you think of him? Do you respect him?"

"Of course, I do," Celeste answered, and that was true. Her admiration grew with every interaction. However, she was realistic. "Bea, if he was interested, shouldn't he be more forthright about it?"

"Ah, Celeste, no man is forthright until he knows he is on firm ground. Especially if he is just discovering he has a heart."

The thought that Oliver had been trying to express his feelings, and that she had been deaf to his words, appalled her. "What do I do, Bea?"

Her friend had a ready answer. "First, stop overthinking."

"How does one do that? Especially if I have been rather callous toward him. I never imagined he might be attracted to me. He's so full of life and honest and wonderful."

"If he is all those things and he genuinely cares, you needn't worry. He will seek you out."

"But what if—"

"What if the moon falls into the ocean? Some things are beyond your control, child. But heed me on this. Stop trying to manage everything."

"How do I do that? I'm responsible for the charity. It is what Father wanted."

"I think your father's true wish was for you, and each of your sisters, to be happy. He has pushed you out of your grief and into the world. His spirit may even be a heavenly hand bringing you and Salcombe together."

Could that be true? Celeste thought back to when she first realized she needed someone to help her start her charity. She had immediately thought of Oliver, even though she hadn't known him. At the time, she'd considered the idea of asking him to be her lead patron as divine inspiration because she had known immediately he would attract attention to her cause.

And then she realized another truth. "I'm in love with him." There, she'd said it, even though she feared she wasn't worthy of such love. "But what if he might have been telling me that he thinks of me as a good friend?"

"That is the risk of love, my dear. One must trust the feelings, even if it turns out they are not returned. That is Shakespeare, and every poet who has ever picked up a quill or pen." Beatrice set down the sherry glass and yawned, covering her mouth as if slightly embarrassed. "I'm for bed. Are you coming?"

"Of course, yes." Tomorrow. She would talk to Oliver in the morning. She'd be honest, or so she promised herself as she followed her friend up the stairs, her mind already roiling with all her fears, doubts, and wants. Oh, yes, she wanted *him*.

Unfortunately, pride was important to her. She didn't want to look a fool. If she misinterpreted his intentions, she might lose her charity's lead patron. Although that might already have happened.

But what if Beatrice was right and he did have feelings for her?

"Celeste, you are doing it again," Beatrice said. The statement startled Celeste into realizing they had reached their bedroom doors.

"I just—" Celeste started, but Beatrice cut her off.

"Darling girl, for once, let yourself believe you are lovable just the way you are. I certainly love you." With those words, Beatrice entered her room.

A maid was waiting for Celeste in her room to help her undress. She let the girl brush out her hair and then dismissed her.

The house was quiet. Celeste blew out the candle, plunging the room into moonlight and shadows. She climbed into bed, knowing she probably would not fall asleep—

A light rap sounded on the door. Celeste sat up, not certain if she'd heard correctly. There was another soft knock.

Celeste found her dressing gown and threw it over her night rail. She cracked open the door, expecting to see Beatrice. Instead, Oliver slipped into her room.

He had taken off his neckcloth, and his shirt hem hung outside his breeches as if he had started to undress, then changed his mind. He still wore his boots. His hair appeared as if he had been dragging his fingers through it. He appeared miserable, his expression tense.

"I need to talk with you about what happened this afternoon," he said. "I feel there is more to be said."

A flood of emotions washed over her, the strongest being hope. A joyous hope.

Suddenly, she understood what Bea had been trying to say. So, she let her heart decide. She grabbed hold of his shirt, the material soft in her clenched fingers, pulled him down, and kissed him with the full passion of her being.

OLIVER WAS STUNNED by her kiss.

Only moments ago, he had believed he was going mad with worry because he'd upset her again. He'd wondered if he would ever do anything right when it came to Celeste. He had no difficulty pleasing other women or maneuvering them toward what he wanted.

But Celeste wasn't other women. She was unique,

special... and he couldn't risk losing her. Because one of the realizations he'd had while he'd been furiously pacing his room was that he loved her. *All* of her—the tilt of her head, the sound of her laugh, her determination, her honesty, her passion.

He'd always assumed the concept of "love" was for fools and poets. He'd thought it a fantasy. However, in this moment, in this kiss, Oliver came face to face with the possibility that *he* was the one who hadn't understood. Nothing in this world meant more to him than Celeste. He wanted her respect, her trust, and for her to *love* him in the way he loved her.

And so, when she pulled him into a kiss, he wrapped his arms around her, lifted her up so that not even her toes touched the floor, and let his kiss speak for him.

Her arms tightened around him. Her breasts pressed against his chest. Oliver carried her to the bed. He had a thought that he would leave her there, but that was not what happened. He was so lost in their kiss that when his legs hit the bed, the two of them fell forward onto the mattress. He twisted at the last moment so that he didn't fall on top of her. Instead, he rolled over onto his back, carrying her with him.

The kiss broke.

She didn't scramble away. Instead, she looked down at him, one hand on the mattress, another on his chest. Her hair created a golden curtain around them.

For a long moment, they stared into each other's eyes.

Gently, he combed the silken strands of her hair back from her face. Then, cradling her face in his palms, he kissed her again, deeper, fuller, the way she deserved to be kissed.

His tongue touched hers. Celeste gave a small start as if

this was unexpected, and then she mimicked him, the tip of her tongue stroking the length of his.

The sensation of it went straight through him to the very willing and ready member pressed against his breeches. He needed to stop this before they went too far. He meant to rise from the bed, but instead, he rolled over, bringing her beneath him. She held fast. Her legs parted, and he found himself nestled against the heart of her.

Oliver thought he would explode. She wasn't being deliberately provocative, just open and straightforward as she always was. She desired him. He could feel the heat of her, even through the layers of her dressing gown and night rail. He wanted to touch her skin.

One more kiss, and he knew he would be powerless to control himself.

CELESTE GAVE her love full rein. It didn't matter what happened on the morrow. She didn't care what anyone thought. Her body sang with the pleasure of touching him. She ached for him and for what only *he* could give her.

He was her forever.

When his lips found her ear, she thought the sensation would send her flying through the ceiling. When his hand covered her hard nipple, and his lips found the other, sucking on it lightly through the material, she gasped and never wanted him to stop. He knew every hidden sweet spot, and she liked letting him explore her body. In turn, she experimented with the tricks he'd just used, enjoying his response to her touch.

She nibbled at the juncture of his neck and chin, reveling in his reaction as he gathered her to him. When she tugged on his shirt, he helped pull it off. She ran her hands over his shoulders and down his back. Her fingers slipped under his breeches and grazed the top of his buttocks. She wanted more. She wanted all he had to offer.

Did she know what she was doing?

Oh, yes.

She let her fingertips travel around his waist until they were tantalizingly close to that hard line of his desire. She found a button. She twisted it. Her movements were clumsy. The button wouldn't give.

He pushed himself up, bracing himself on his forearms. "We should stop." His voice sounded husky.

The moonlight hit the hard, masculine planes of his chest and shoulders as he started to move away from her. She threw an arm around him. "No."

"Celeste—" he started in a warning voice, but then the tips of her fingers slipped beneath the waist of his breeches and found the smooth, velvety head of his maleness. He sucked in his breath. A surge of warmth and need gathered between her legs. She moved her hips, her breasts had gone hard and full, and she yearned for him.

He began unbuttoning his breeches. She bit back a moan of desire as his manhood sprang to life, finally free of restrictions. He levered up and sat on the edge of the bed to remove his boots. First, one hit the floor, then the other. Celeste ran a hand up and down his arm, needing to touch him.

He stood. His breeches joined his boots, and he was gloriously naked.

Celeste rose from the bed and struggled out of her dressing gown. He reached to help her, and then he pulled the nightdress over her head.

She sucked in her breath, shy at being stripped of all artifice in front of him. She was being too bold—

"You are beautiful," he whispered.

She might have laughed at such a statement, except he looked at her as if her body was a marvel, as if looking at her *pleased* him. And for the first time, she believed she did possess beauty. Her heart filled with joy and she fell into his arms.

It felt good to have her naked skin against his. Their kisses became more passionate, more demanding. He covered her with his body, and she cradled him between her legs.

His manhood pressed against her. Instinctively, she braced herself and then slowly drew in her breath as he entered her.

This was what they claimed was the secret to life. *This* was what the poets lauded and women whispered over.

And *this* was a bit of a disappointment.

Her body stretched to accommodate him. The feeling was alien, not uncomfortable, but not, well, she hadn't known what to expect.

"Are you all right?" he asked.

She nodded, holding her breath.

"You are lying," he said with a chuckle. Inside her, she felt his manhood move with the motion of his laughter, and it startled her.

She released her breath. "I felt that."

"You are going to feel more." He slid an arm under her back, bringing her into his protective embrace. "This may hurt, Celeste. I'm sorry. But the pain should not last."

"I trust you."

He kissed her, a quick, hard kiss that distracted her as he suddenly thrust deep.

There was a sharp pain. She jerked as if to escape. He held her fast, not moving, as if he were attempting to absorb her discomfort with his own body. To her surprise, the pain quickly ebbed. She discovered she liked having him inside her.

"All good?" he rasped out.

She nodded, her breasts moving against his chest. He began rocking against her, his thrusts gentle at first but taking on more force as she began rising up to meet him.

Every time he touched the center of her, she felt tiny starbursts going off. She found herself striving for them, wanting more. Always more.

His heavy breathing matched her own. Her legs now hugged his hips, pulling him into her. Deeper. *Deeper*. And then—

A sharp, bright pinnacle of emotion seized her. Wave after wave of sensation flowed through her.

He knew what was happening. His movements became more directed, harder, faster. Once, twice, and the third thrust sent him to his own satisfaction.

With a sense of wonder, Celeste realized this was what they meant when they said that two should become one. She was one with Oliver. She was his.

He whispered her name. It sounded like a benediction, and then he collapsed over to one side of her body so that she would not have to bear the brunt of his weight. She made a disconsolate sound as he slipped out of her, his seed spent. He reached for the counterpane and pulled it over them. They lay entwined, Celeste lost in wave after rippling wave of pleasure.

Oliver pressed his lips to her temple. His arm came around her beneath the coverlet. "I shouldn't have done that."

She kissed his forearm. "Yes, you should have." Her voice had a purr to it.

"Celeste, I meant—"

"I know what you meant," she interrupted him. "It was amazing. The best experience of my life."

"*You* are the best thing I've experienced in my life." He kissed her cheek, her nose, her mouth.

She curled up against him, needing his warmth. "I like you, too." She rubbed her palm against his skin at the hip. He was saying something to her, but she didn't listen. She didn't want to think. She didn't want to worry. She just wanted to love. In this moment, her love for him was all that mattered.

In that fashion, she fell into one of the deepest, most peaceful sleeps she'd ever experienced. She had found where she belonged—beside him. Wrapped in his arms, she dreamed of his kisses, of him saying he loved her and all would be well, that she could trust him.

Yes, trust. Love was trust, and she loved him very much.

THE NEXT MORNING, she woke to find herself in an empty bed.

10

The hour was late. Celeste rarely slept as late as it was now. Nor did she understand why Oliver hadn't woken her. She rationalized that he hadn't wanted to disturb her sleep or was being considerate of her reputation and did not want to be caught in her bed. That would not be a good thing. What if Beatrice discovered he had been in her room all night?

A little voice told her Bea would not bat a lash. Or carry tales.

Perhaps he was worried about the servants' gossip? His staff seemed well trained, but one never knew.

Without summoning a maid, she dressed and quickly braided her hair, not bothering with pins and nonsense. She wanted to see Oliver.

She needed to gauge his reaction to last night. How did he feel this morning? The fear that she'd been just another trophy for a man known for his skills in seducing women reared its ugly head.

The hallway was quiet. She went downstairs to find Beatrice sipping tea in the breakfast room.

Her friend looked up with a bright smile. "You are up early. So was the duke. In fact, he has already left."

"He left? To go riding?"

"No, he left on some business. He was in quite a hurry and in remarkable spirits. I told him I hadn't seen him so lively. When I asked what he was about, he said it was a secret." Beatrice shrugged. "He said he had to leave right that moment so he would be back in time for the ball tomorrow evening."

Celeste carefully sat in the nearest chair. She nodded when a footman offered to pour her a cup of the strong black tea she favored. She took a deep breath, then released it. She did not touch the tea. She didn't trust herself to hold the cup steady. "Did he say anything more?"

Had he left a message for her?

Bea shook her head. "Just that he had to dash. I told him you would be disappointed to miss saying goodbye to him. He told me he would make it up to you later." She held up the page of the paper she had been reading. "Last evening's paper claims your subscription ball will be one of the top events of the Season. Salcombe's staff seems to be doing everything right. You will be happy to hear that one editor wrote about how the pensions given to soldiers gravely injured in war are not enough. He recommends that everyone support the charity. Of course, the papers give all credit to Salcombe, but what do we care so long as the charity is a success? Your father would be very proud of you."

At one time, honoring her father's bequest had been everything Celeste had wished to accomplish. Now, she listened to Beatrice as if from a distance.

Then she became angry.

He'd left. He'd treated her like some doxy, and not a

Harrington of the proud House of Kenbrooks. She pictured taking one of the iron pikes that decorated Fenmere Park's entrance hall and skewering him with it.

The butler, Avery, entered the room. He carried a folded and sealed note on a silver salver, Muggins following on his heels. The terrier stopped in the doorway, looked around, and then sniffed as if annoyed Oliver wasn't in the room. He turned and pranced back down the hall. Avery shook his head with a smile and offered the salver to Celeste. "My lady, this is from the duke."

Relief flooded her. He had not forgotten her. She took the missive and cracked the wax seal.

Oliver had very distinctive handwriting. It was slanted and bold. He was left-handed, she realized. She had not noticed that before.

She looked the note. *All will be well. I shall see you tomorrow evening when I return. S.*

"Is everything all right?" Beatrice asked.

All will be well.

The words he'd spoken in her dream, and now here was the same promise in his handwriting. What did he mean?

Celeste folded the note, lowered her hand to her lap, and crushed the foolscap in her fist. Relief changed into bitter disappointment. This was all the man had to say after she given him not only her body but her heart? She had expected more. She wanted more.

And the duke had given all he was willing to give, apparently. After all, he was the Dragon, a man who broke women's hearts for sport. Well, now he had her name on his list. What had been life altering to her had obviously been just another romp for him.

Pride came to her rescue. She wouldn't let Bea or the servants see that anything was amiss. No, she'd save her sharp words for tomorrow evening when the Dragon expected her to be smiling and compliant.

For the briefest moment, she remembered him stroking her hair as she fell asleep with her head on his chest. His touch had been gentle and loving.

Or had she imagined those emotions because she'd let down her guard?

"When are we leaving?" she abruptly asked Beatrice.

Avery answered, "It will take an hour to ready the coach. I was about to ask when you wished to return to Town? His Grace said you may stay here as his guests as long as you wish."

Celeste stood. She was no longer shaky; she was furious. "Have the coach brought round as soon as possible. Excuse me, Bea, but I need to see that my things are packed. We will leave as soon as possible."

"Aren't you going to eat first?" Beatrice asked.

"I'm not hungry."

Up in her room, she set about folding her clothes into her portmanteau that she had set on the bed. The maid offered to help with packing, but Celeste sent her away. She needed to be alone before she was betrayed by the doubt and hurt she attempted to hold at bay.

The moment the door closed behind the servant, Celeste almost crumpled to the floor. She wrapped her arms around her waist in an attempt to hold herself together. She remembered him deep inside her, connecting them in both body and spirit, and she wanted to hate him—

Except, she didn't.

Nor would she give in to crippling self-recriminations. She was not sorry she had given him her trust. She had been honest in her emotions. Her love for him was strong and clear. She'd given herself freely. Her only sin, she realized, was expecting him to be something he wasn't.

Besides, if he was the sort of man to run off, she had no need for him.

The thought gave her courage, a courage she hadn't believed she possessed. A sense of calm fell over her. She straightened her body and took several deep breaths.

She was determined to honor her father's belief in her. She now understood the charity was something true to her heart, just as he'd directed. Did it hurt that Oliver had left her? Absolutely. But his actions would not deter her from her course.

Celeste had dared to go after the one man who had captured her interest, and she'd not apologize for being true to her heart. Instead, she decided, the time had come for the Dragon to learn that not all women played his games.

THE PAPERS WERE NOT wrong about the anticipation for the subscription ball. Celeste's sisters claimed it was all anyone could talk about. Since the duke's staff had taken care of all the details, Celeste didn't even have the ball to fret over. She was just expected to show up.

She tried to focus on the charity's success. Many wounded soldiers would be helped. Lord Masick's property would eventually provide dozens of homes for them and their pets. It was going to be all that she had envisioned.

Celeste was frustrated that, in spite of her proud promises to herself, she was so weak as to hope Oliver would call and explain himself. As the hours passed without word, her imagination created all sorts of mean-spirited reasons for his callous disregard. There were moments when her bravado waivered, when she was certain if he had physically stabbed her in the heart, she could not be in more pain.

However, she would survive this. She would carry on. She was a Harrington. She dressed for the ball in an indigo gown that brought out the green and golden flecks in her eyes. This was the best she'd ever looked and the color made her feel powerful.

It also helped her spirits that her brother, the Duke of Kenbrooks and his duchess, Felicia, arrived, surprising everyone. The couple preferred Fenmere Park and rarely came to Town. They hadn't even sent word to expect them. They were both in great spirits and obviously thought Celeste should be as well.

"Father would have been so proud of you, Cece," her brother said, using her nickname.

Celeste accepted her brother's praise as a talisman to help her through this night. She and her family, with the absence of their mother, who was dining before the ball with Lady Redhill, left for the event.

At the Duke of Salcombe's home, all were in a rush to finish the last details before the guests arrived. Celeste braced herself for her meeting with the duke. A harried Mr. Peters herded her toward the ballroom entrance. "You will be in the receiving line with His Grace."

"No, I won't," Celeste informed him, but before she could sail away with her head held high, the hairs at the nape of her neck tingled with anticipation. The air seemed to shift, and she caught the scent of shaving soap—one she knew well since she'd spent a night breathing in every inch of Oliver.

She turned. He was coming down the hall toward her.

The world, her family's chattering, the servants' movements, and the musicians tuning their instruments faded until there was only the duke. The smile on his handsome face was welcoming. His eyes were warm with what appeared to be happiness at seeing her.

At first, his reaction was confusing. Her hands curled into fists, as she remembered drawing him into her room, into her bed, into her body. Her heart pounded, and she found it hard to breathe. Did he expect her to be grateful that he had not cut her out completely? That he'd let her stand in the receiving line while everyone lauded his great insight into the dishonorable pittance the country was giving men who had sacrificed their limbs and futures for its king?

Except, suddenly, she realized she didn't care who was given credit for the charity, not really. Her goal had been to see a wrong righted. And so it would be, eventually.

However, as he approached, she mourned what she had lost. *Him.* The man she had dared to trust with her love.

The duke stopped in front of her. "Are you pleased? We are the talk of the Town."

Celeste looked up at him and realized she couldn't fake pleasantries. Not with him. "I was such an easy conquest, wasn't I?" She shouldn't have said it.

Her twin, standing close to her, overhead. George stiffened and moved closer to her. "What is it, Cece? Has something happened?"

"Nothing of importance," Celeste answered and gave Salcombe her back. She was done with him. She might have left except that the first guests began to arrive. To her annoyance, it was Lord and Lady Redhill and her mother.

The duke's hand caught hers before she could think of her next move. His gloved grip was tight as he pulled her into the nearest side room. He closed the door behind them, his expression concerned.

"What has happened? You're angry with me?"

Pride kept her from bursting into tears. "I refuse to expend that much emotion on you. We need to return. Guests are arriving."

His brows came together. "Are you upset that everyone credits me with the idea of founding the charity? Celeste, I acknowledge that people should not ignore that this is your idea. And they won't be able to after they see this." He pulled a vellum card from inside his jacket pocket and offered it to her.

In the finest engraving, it was a program of events for the evening, including the introduction of the Patroness of Our Brave Soldiers, Lady Celeste Harrington. His name was not on the card. He was giving her all the credit.

Celeste frowned at the words. The letters seemed to spin a little, and she closed her eyes. "I—" She started and then stopped. Her pride didn't want him to know how deeply he had hurt her. But to be silent felt dishonest. Cowardly even.

She loved him and... and...

Annoying tears pooled in her eyes. "You left."

He leaned down to her, tilting her face up. A tear escaped, and he gently wiped it from her cheek as if it was the most important task he could perform. "I woke you to let you know I had to leave but that I would return."

She thought of her dream. Of how deeply she'd slept. "I don't remember."

"I also wrote you a note."

"That all would be well? What was 'well' about you leaving?"

"Celeste, I had to leave. Otherwise, I could not have traveled to Surrey to see your brother and return in time for this evening's ball."

"Why would you go to see him in Surrey?"

He took both of her gloved hands in his own. She noticed he seemed surprisingly nervous, and then he knelt before her. "Celeste, would you—?" He paused. "This is harder than I thought it would be because you could very well refuse me."

She straightened. "Refuse you?" He now had her full attention.

"My lady, may I have your hand in marriage? Will you be my duchess?"

"Why?" The word burst out of her before she could question the wisdom of it. "You could do so much better."

"Oh, no, I can't. Or are you are telling me no?" His brows came together. "You do not care for me? Celeste, *I love you.* You've changed my life. You've made me a different person. Any respect I receive is because of you—"

She launched herself into his arms. He caught her and rose, carrying her with him. He held her fast but not as tightly as she was holding him.

"I love you. I adore you," she said against his hard chest, the velvet of his evening finery soft against her cheek.

"Does that mean you will be my duchess?"

"Yes, yes, yes, and *yes.* I was heartbroken when I feared you didn't care for me."

"I tried to wake you. I wrote a note—"

"We shall work on your note writing skills later. Right now, I want you to kiss me."

And so, he did.

Their kiss was broken by a knock on the door. George's voice called, "Cece, is everything all right? Do you need me?"

"Everything has never been better," Celeste vowed.

"The guests are piling up at the door, and Mr. Peters is frantic to start the receiving line. Mother is complaining bitterly."

"We shall be right there," Oliver called. He kissed her again on the top of her head.

Celeste smiled and took a moment to realign the folds of his neckcloth, which she had ruffled. He was incredibly handsome, and he was hers. "You love me," she whispered.

"And you love me," he answered.

"More than you can imagine."

His answer was to kiss her again, deeply, fully. "We shall marry by special license," he promised. "I don't think I can wait for the banns to be announced." And then he held out his gloved hand. "Shall we greet the subscribers of your charity, my future duchess?"

She placed her palm in his. "*Our* charity," she corrected, but he shook his head.

"This is yours, Celeste, and I'll not take it from you. But I will stand beside you to offer support and respect for your courage and your willingness to correct what others have ignored. It is a great accomplishment. Let's celebrate."

And celebrate they did. Not only did they sign on many subscribers to the charity, but no one who saw them that evening failed to recognize they were in love.

AND SO...

George had never seen her twin happier or more completely in her element. Cece truly believed in the mission of her charity and handled the questions and comments from many of the titled guests with a confidence she'd not demonstrated before.

What pleased George even more was the way Salcombe looked at his bride-to-be. He'd proudly announced to the assembled company that Celeste had agreed to marry him. Someone in the crowd had called out, "The Dragon had finally been tamed."

Salcombe had readily agreed... and George couldn't help but feel a touch envious of her twin. It would be lovely to have a man as handsome and generous adore her, too.

At that moment, one of the duke's footmen approached her. He was holding a small silver salver, carrying it carefully as he avoided one of the guests' elbows that came back suddenly. She waited for him, knowing deep in her bones what was about to happen. After all, she had seen this scene play out for her sister Honoria and for Celeste.

"Lady Georgiana?"

"Yes."

He held out a silver tray holding a single red envelope. Her father's task for her.

"My turn," she murmured, reaching for the envelope.

"I beg your pardon, my lady?"

George shook her head and broke the wax seal.

Enjoy the next installment of the Busty Bodice Club, CURVES FOR THE SILVER FOX DUKE by Tracy Sumner https://books2read.com/CFTSilverFoxDuke

AUTHOR'S NOTE

Celeste's instinct to protect animals as well as humans was not off the mark for her time in history. In 1824, the Reverend Arthur Boome, a longtime advocate of treating animals with kindness, chaired a meeting to form the Society for the Prevention of Cruelty to Animals. The founding members were men of status. No women attended, although I suspect there were strong female voices prodding the gentleman into action.

I like to think Oliver took a seat at that table.

Today, we know the organization they created as the Royal Society for the Prevention of Cruelty to Animals (RSPCA), and it is the oldest animal welfare organization in the world.

ABOUT THE AUTHOR

Cathy Maxwell has written forty some historical romances, hit the New York Times and USA Today lists, been nominated for--and won--some very nice awards, made dynamite writing friends, and has had the time of her life. If you yak at her on Facebook, she usually yaks back. Anything to procrastinate!

To read excerpts from her books and to sign up for her newsletter for updates and so on and so forth, please check out www.cathymaxwell.com

ALSO BY CATHY MAXWELL

WWW.CATHYMAXWELL.COM

<u>Single Title</u>

All Thing Beautiful

Treasured Vows

You and No Other

Falling in Love Again

When Dreams Come True

Because of You

The Wedding Wager

The Lady is Tempted

Adventures of a Scottish Heiress

The Seduction of an English Lady

<u>Marriage series</u>

Married in Haste

A Scandalous Marriage

The Marriage Contract

<u>Cameron Sisters series</u>

The Temptation of a Proper Governess

The Price of Indiscretion

In the Bed of a Duke
Bedding the Heiress
In a Highlander's Bed

Seduction and Scandal series
A Seduction at Christmas
The Earl Claims His Wife
The Marriage Ring
His Christmas Pleasure
The Seduction of Scandal

The Chattan Curse series
Lyon's Bride
The Scottish Witch
The Devil's Heart

The Brides of Wishmore Series
The Bride Said No
The Bride Said Maybe
The Groom Said Yes

Marrying the Duke Series
The Match of the Century
Fairest of Them All
A Date at the Altar

The Spinster Heiresses
If Ever I Should Love You
A Match Made in Bed
The Duke That I Marry

The Logical Man's Guide to Dangerous Women
His Secret Mistress

Her First Desire
His Lessons on Love

The Gambler's Daughters
A Kiss in the Moonlight
One Dangerous Night
A Touch of Steele

The Busty Bodice Club
Curves for the Rakish Duke

THE BUSTY BODICE CLUB

Seven Authors, Eight Heroines, One Unforgettable Club.

Add in a father's final wish: live boldly, love recklessly, and never hide the curves of your lives—or your bodies.

From scandalous portraits and secret wagers...to daring rescues and forbidden kisses...the Busty Bodice Club isn't just about finding love. It's about embracing every lush curve, every wild desire, and every reckless chance at happiness.

Curves for the Grumpy Duke
by Eliana Piers
https://books2read.com/CFTGrumpyDuke

Curves for the Rakish Duke
by Cathy Maxwell
https://books2read.com/CFTRakishDuke

Curves for the Silver Fox Duke
by Tracy Sumner
https://books2read.com/CFTSilverFoxDuke

Curves for the Beastly Duke
by Annabelle Anders
https://books2read.com/CFTBeastlyDuke

Curves for the Betrothed Duke
by Robyn Dehart
https://books2read.com/CFTBetrothedDuke

Curves for the Scandalous Duke
by Kathleen Ayers
https://books2read.com/CFTScandalousDuke

Curves for the Secret Duke
by Janna MacGregor
https://books2read.com/CFTSecretDuke

CURVES
GRUMPY
DUKE
ELIANA
PIERS
CURVES
RAKISH
DUKE
CATHY
MAXWELL
CURVES
SILVER FOX
DUKE
TRACY
SUMNER
BUSTY
BODICE
CLUB
CURVES
BUSTY
DUKE
ANNABELLE
ANDERS
CURVES
BETROTHED
DUKE
ROBYN
DEHART
CURVES
SCANDALOUS
DUKE
KATHLEEN
AYERS
CURVES
SECRET
DUKE
JANNA
MACGREGOR

www.ingramcontent.com/pod-product-compliance
Lightning Source LLC
LaVergne TN
LVHW010938110826
845149LV00013B/2663

* 9 7 9 8 9 9 3 0 9 4 1 1 3 *